It's Just One Thing After Another!

The New Abby Marshall and
Donny Weston Thriller
By

David O'Neil

Argus Enterprises International, Inc.
New Jersey***North Carolina

It's Just One Thing After Another! ©
2013, All rights reserved by David
O'Neil.

A-Argus Better Book Publishers, LLC

For information:
A-Argus Better Book Publishers, LLC
9001 Ridge Hill Street
Kernersville, North Carolina 27285
www.a-argusbooks.com

ISBN: 978-0-6157716-9-4
ISBN 0-6157716-9-6

Book Cover designed by Dubya
Printed in the United States of America

Chapter One

So this is America, thought Abby Marshall as she and Donny Weston eventually found their way through the intricacies of immigration and passport control at Logan International Airport, Boston. "A gift from a grateful Government," was the way Jonathon Glynn had put it.

Donny's reaction had been cynical. "Beware of Greeks bearing gifts."

Jonathon Glynn, who served with M16, was a friend of Donny's father. He had been their mentor throughout the past three years, since they first became involved in the conflicts that had tested their courage and survival skills to the limit.

They had taken a year out from University to try to remove the threat of reaction from enemies that still posed a threat to both of them. The months of frantic action in Europe had entailed conflict with ex-Speznatz mercenaries. It had been dangerous and exhausting for them both.

Having survived, and succeeded in removing that last threat, they had faced the prospect of occupying the rest of the year with a certain amount of concern. That was when Jonathon Glynn had arrived with the offer of a six-week all-expenses-paid trip across America.

Despite his misgivings, Donny was cautiously optimistic as they discussed their first full day in the United States of America. Abby had arranged for them to join a morning tour of Harvard, and, with Donny very much in mind, an afternoon tour of the *USS Constitution*—the three-mast 19th Century frigate moored as a museum in Boston Harbor.

The feeling of awe as he walked through the entrance to Harvard was unexpected. Despite coming from a rather more modern University in England, Donny Weston did not expect to feel the same sort of atmosphere that he felt when visiting Abby at her college in Oxford.

The guide for the tour was enthusiastic and knowledgeable, and his detailed dissertation on the characters that had created this University made it clear why this establishment had attained and maintained its august reputation. The duo lagged behind while Abby read a wall plaque.

They were reminded by their guide, who coughed irritably to get their attention to continue with the tour.

"The others are waiting," the guide said. "Please keep up. There is more to see and time is getting on."

Abby flashed a smile. "I am so sorry. I was so impressed by the history and the feeling of antiquity in the college that I got carried away. I won't let it happen again."

Mollified, the guide led them to the others in the party and the tour continued.

In Boston Harbor they had visited the *USS Constitution,* a visit Donny had promised himself as soon as the cross-country trip had been suggested. The beautifully preserved ship had lived up to expectations as far as Donny was concerned. For Abby the people on the tour were the greatest interest. Though she was interested in the ship generally, the wide diversity of visitors—tourists from overseas and other parts of the USA—was more or less equally spread. She shrugged, thinking how very different things could be between countries with so much in common.

Later, as they followed route I-95 south through Rhode Island on their way to New York, Abby commented. "It's funny. I've heard people say many times how different things can be between Britain and the United States, but until now I thought they were just being clever. You know, showing off, boasting about their trip to the '*States*.' The fact that they had actually been there and knew what they were talking about."

"So, what's so funny?"

"I've come to the conclusion that perhaps they did know what they were talking about. Those people today, on the tour, they were all so earnest, and yes, the place was interesting, but I felt that I was not reacting with the sort of respect that I should have."

Donny, who had been far more interested in the tour of the *USS Constitution,* thought about it and decided that discretion was probably the way to go. "Well, remember you started your degree in Oxford, where the place reeks of antiquity. Poor old Harvard was a late starter by comparison. Considering that, I think they show up pretty well here in terms of education, and if the chance were offered, I would be interested in spending some time here.

"I was actually thinking about the tour of the ship. There were people from all over on that tour. There was even a man in a suit with a briefcase. What are the odds?"

"He was probably killing time between meetings," Danny suggested.

"Perhaps; now I think about it, he did seem a little stressed." Abby let it drop.

"You must admit this is quite an exciting place to be." Danny swerved to avoid a panel van that was crowding them toward the crash barrier.

The van veered toward them again and Donny braked sharply, allowing the van to move across in front of their rental car. The van accelerated, still weaving slightly, and Donny increased speed once more. "There, you see what I mean. It can be quite exciting here."

They pulled into a motel on the outskirts of West Warwick. There was the usual assembly of eating places and a Wal-Mart, in addition to the motel.

"I've had enough driving for today, so I have made an executive decision. We stay here tonight and we won't eat at MacDonald's."

Abby looked at him and grinned. "You can be so masterful at times." She opened the door and leapt out of the car. Her bag was on the back seat and grabbing it she said, "I'll get the room. You get the bags."

Donny looked appreciatively at her rear view as she walked across the parking area toward the motel entrance.

He hauled their two overnight bags from the trunk and blipped the key—locking the car—and turned to follow Abby. He was in time to see her kick a young man between the legs. A second man was on the ground, shaking his head, looking dazed. A third was creeping toward Abby from behind. Donny ran across the parking area still carrying the two bags. As he approached the scene he tossed the bag in his right hand at the creeping man behind Abby. It caught him behind his left ear. He stumbled and fell on his face. The bag rolled past him as he lay there.

Abby turned and looked at the third man. "What is this all about, do you think?"

Donny said, "They probably saw what I saw when you walked away from me."

Abby looked at him sharply. "What do you mean?"

"You do have a sexy rear view, you know."

The first man was back on his feet, so Abby turned toward him. He held up his hands in protest. "No, no, they said this was a pushover. They made a mistake." He turned and ran off.

The man who had been kicked was hobbling off in the other direction, still nursing his crotch. Donny's victim was beginning to stir but still looked dazed, so it was to him that Donny turned. "So, what was that all about?"

"Wha... what do you mean?"

"Why were you attacking my friend, is what I mean." Donny lifted the other bag and started to swing it.

"No. Don't!" the man said. "It was just one of those things. The guys saw you when they passed you in their van. They said you got out of their way like a pussy, so when they saw you pull in here they thought they would have a little fun. That was all."

"Who are these guys, then?"

"The two who got away." The man was talking his head off now, eager to please.

"You are lying!" Donny lifted the bag again but Abby stepped forward.

"I'll work him over a little. He will be happy to talk when I've finished with him."

"Hey, lady, I'm just the hired help. I don't know nothing!"

"Well, I'll rough him up a little, or maybe we'll just turn him over to the law. There's a cop coming into the car park just now."

"Gimme a break, you two. I've just got out of the joint. Those guys will have me back in before I know what's happening."

"So who set up this little game, then?"

The man looked sullenly at the pair. "A guy in the café there saw you come in and said he would give us fifty dollars to tousle you up a little; nothing serious, no broken bones, just bruises, maybe a bloody nose."

You are playing games. Get the cop, Donny." Abby sounded serious.

"Okay. He said to hurt you so you would go back to where you came from."

"What did this guy look like?"

"You won't believe me if I tell you."

"Try me!" Said Abby,

"Yul Brunner!"

"Yeah, nice one now. Really, what did he look like?"

"I told you, you wouldn't believe me." The man said in an aggrieved tone. "He looked like Yul Brunner—bald head and darkish skin—like he had seen too much sun, y'know?"

They let the man go.

Abby checked them into a room and claimed the whirlpool bath. Donny settled for a shower, and then chased Abby out of the bath because he was hungry.

In the restaurant they sat down to eat. While Donny looked at the menu, Abby looked around. "Well, well!" She said. "Look who is here."

Donny looked up to see what she was talking about. Across the room sat a well-dressed man in a grey suit, he was completely bald, he turned while they were watching him.

"Yul Brunner!" Abby said. "Would you believe it? Shall we talk to him, I wonder?"

"No!" Donny said. "He does not know that we know he put those men onto us. Let's keep it that way."

"There's something about him, the way he looks. He is not quite…." She hesitated. "Remember the Russians in France."

Donny looked at her pityingly. "How could I forget? I seem to recall spending much of my time dodging their bullets."

"But, don't you see? He is like them. I think he is Russian. If he is, that could be the reason he put those men onto us."

"That is what I call a stretch. I think I would have remembered him if I had seen him in France."

"I'm not saying that he was there. I mean he may be a relative of one that was there. They did have pictures of us after all."

"Well I am hungry. So let's eat. Tomorrow we'll go to New York and on Saturday we will be heading west for San Francisco. I am looking forward to it and I am not going to let some Russian Mafioso spoil our holiday."

The Peugeot rental car cruised into New York in the late afternoon, luckily before the real rush hour began. Following the instruction of the GPS they reached their hotel and Donny sent the car diving down into the underground car park that serviced the patrons of the Ramada Plaza Inn on 8th Avenue.

It would not have been the first choice of the young couple if they had been travelling at their own expense. As it was, the entire six-week break was with the compliments of a department of the EU Government.

As a result of their activities over the past three years, several organizations had ceased activity and a considerable amount of overt illegal activity had come to light. According to Jonathon Glynn, friend of the family and member of one of the alphabet departments of British Security, the reward had been granted because the activities of the young couple interfered with too many financial schemes. Their presence was becoming embarrassing. The grant of an educational trip to the USA meant they would be out of the way. Too many people high in the Euro-administration felt their images might suffer, if the stir they had created revealed too much.

So, still with time to spare before they resumed their university studies, they accepted the offer of travel and expenses and set off. They were three days into their break and beginning to really enjoy the relaxed atmosphere they had encountered in the US so far.

From their room they could see the vista of New York City. There was a city map in the drawer and on it they picked out a route to Times Square and Central Park. Tomorrow they would see the Empire State Building and go to visit the Statue of Liberty.

Abby said, "I know it sounds corny but, until I have seen it, I won't really feel I've been to New York." She looked at Donny to see if he was going to pull her leg about her comment.

Donny lifted his eyes from the map and looked back. "Quite right too. How could we visit New York without doing the tour! Anyway, now I'm ready to eat and I fancy trying a deli in Times Square. Are you in?"

"Ready when you are!" Abby bounced off the bed and found her trainers. She slipped them on, stood up and spun around in front of him. "Will I do?" She said with a smile.

Donny growled, "Anytime!" He reached out to grab her. She eluded him and made for the door. "Let's eat. I'm starving." She was through the door and into the hallway before he could catch her. Laughing together, they boarded the elevator and descended to the lobby.

The streets were still busy with people as they went out into 8th Avenue. On the sidewalk they turned north for some blocks to the New York City Church where they turned and walked through to Broadway. They found a deli but settled for Italian instead, and ate in a noisy atmosphere of spaghetti and Italian voices shouting orders and comments and a lot of laughter. Within minutes of their arrival they were in conversation with the couple at the next table and, because of their English accents, soon found they had invitations from all over New York from the customers who insisted on joining the conversation.

After much longer than they had anticipated they tore themselves away from their new friends and made their way down Broadway. It was now getting dark and the crowds had thinned out.

"Home time, I guess." Abby said with a yawn.

"Yes. It has been a long day," Donny agreed. Lifting his hand he flagged a passing cab.

Back in their room Donny followed Abby through the door. On the floor was a white card. Abby picked it up and looked at it. Without a word she passed it to Donny.

There was a name on the card. Alex Randall. He turned it over. It said, *'call me'* there was a cell phone number written, then *'Jonathon sends his regards.'*

Donny looked at Abby; she returned the look and shrugged.

Although they had been through some pretty traumatic experiences and were looking forward to the relaxation ahead of them, neither could ignore the prickle of excitement that the thought of action brought.

Donny tapped out the number on his cell phone.

"Randall! Who is this?"

"My name is Weston. You left your card?"

"Ah yes. Is Abby Marshall with you?"

"Yes. So what is this all about?"

"Oh. It's nothing at all, really. Jonathon asked me to contact you and see that you are all right. Can we meet?"

"Do you think it necessary?"

"It's nothing like that. I just wanted to meet, to put a face to you both. Jonathon has told me of some of your adventures in Europe, and if you would like, I thought we could have lunch in the Park tomorrow?"

Donny looked at Abby, covered the mouthpiece and said, "Lunch in the Park tomorrow?"

She shrugged. "Why not?"

"Right! One o'clock at the open air restaurant in the Park."

"I'll know you!" Randall said and rang off.

Donny put the phone down and sprang onto the bed growling and grabbing Abby hungrily.

"You escaped me before, but nobody gets away from the masked avenger."

The pair collapsed on the bed laughing helplessly.

***

Alex Randall looked and sounded like a movie FBI man. He was around six feet tall with greying hair and regular features. He was wearing a sports coat and slacks with an open-neck shirt with button-down collar. He smiled easily and greeted them warmly.

They sat down and looked at the menu, both electing to have the soup and a Caesar salad.

"Is there a problem?" Abby said directly.

Alex looked at them both and made his decision. "I did not wish to interfere with your holiday. But now I have met you, maybe I will." He held his hand up to stop the questions trembling on Abby's lips. "Wait, Jonathon spoke to me yesterday for the second time in the past two weeks. We are old friends, having worked together in some odd places.

"When he knew you were coming here he rang me and asked if I could keep a fatherly eye on you, just in case problems arose."

He took a bite of his club sandwich and concentrated on his eating for a few moments. Then he continued. "I got a second call yesterday. He had received information that there were several ex-members of Speznatz here in USA now involved in the local crime scene. Apparently they had been part of a bigger operation that ran in the Euro-zone. The people here had been sent to ensure that the US end of the operation did not foul up. It seems that the 'Godfather' here had a reputation for holding his partners to ransom over contracts. He would sign. seal and deliver, then-- once the routine had been established—he would change the rules. Deny all product until a new more lucrative deal was struck.

"The Russians were here to dissuade him of any attempt of this kind. They had to kill him in the end and take over the business themselves. You will appreciate that having taken all this trouble to smooth out operations this end, you two came along and caused the entire European end to go up in smoke."

Donny said slowly, "Oops. But why?"

Abby said seriously, "Are you suggesting that they may attempt to delete us, how do they put it, 'with extreme prejudice'?"

"Something like that." Alex Randall did not sound as if he was joking.

"You have still not explained why they should be interested in us?" Donny persisted.

"We can only presume from what has happened so far, that someone doesn't like you. At that point with these people all bets are off, and you go on the list."

"Are you suggesting that we cut our holiday short and go home?" Abby sounded a little tense.

Donny hastily interjected his own comment. "We have just arrived and we will not be leaving on some rumor cooked up between Jonathon and you."

Abby nodded in agreement.

Alex Randall sighed. "Jonathon said this would happen. He also said if you took that line I would have to have you deported to get rid of you." He held his hands up once more. "It's all right. That is not going to happen. But in that case...." He reached into his pocket and pulled out two laminated cards. He read them himself then handed one to each of them. They bore the seal of the United States Government, and they entitled Donald Weston and Abigail Marshall, to the assistance and protection of all law enforcement agencies in the United States, and permitted the holders to carry concealed weapons for the purpose of self-protection and protection of others. They were signed by the Director of the Federal Bureau of Investigations.

"There is a reputable gun shop downtown. I suggest you pay a call as soon as possible, preferably immediately after our lunch. If it's alright, I will personally escort you and place myself at your disposal for advice as to make, size, calibre and anything else I can suggest at the time. Tomorrow you will be on your own."

They finished their lunch each deep in their own thoughts, and afterwards joined Alex Randall in his car for the journey to the downtown gun shop.

The proprietor was a tall stringy individual with a Southern accent who greeted Alex as if he knew him. He gave them both a smile that seemed to split his face in two and swept them behind the counter of the store to a door marked, 'Range'. Alex had explained what was needed.

Max flung the door of the range open. "Let's go downstairs and see what we can do for you here." he said.

"Charlie!" He called to his assistant. "Look after the store."

The basement was set up as a shooting range with the traditional targets and ranges marked, and three small booths for the shooters to attend to their targets and reloads.

Max smiled and took Abby to the end booth, passed out ear defenders to them all and lifted a Colt frontier model from a rack, which opened to his touch.

He smiled and offered the long, heavy weapon to Abby.

Donny grinned, but kept quiet as Abby fumbled a little and seemed put out by the weight of the long-barrelled pistol

"How do...."

Max said "You just pull the hammer back, point and shoot."

"Like this?" Abby turned to the range targets, pulling the hammer smoothly back and fired once, twice, three times, then fanned the hammer with her left hand firing the other three bullets in rapid succession.

Max looked stunned for a moment, then he whooped out loud. "You got me there, Ma'am. Where did you learn to shoot like that?"

"Donny taught me," she said simply.

Max rolled back the target. One shot was low and to the left, the others were all in the inner ring in a three-inch group.

"I wasn't really aiming." Abby said. "The trigger was lighter than I expected so I had to adjust."

Alex shook his head in disgust. "Damn. Jonathon didn't mention this."

Max brought out a .375 magnum which he passed to Donny with a raised eyebrow.

Donny lifted it single-handed and fired three double-action, then switched hands and fired three single-action with his left hand. The target was without a centre section, all six bullets had grouped about the bull.

"Shit!" Max said. "What will it be?"

"Walther PPK 7,65mm, waistband holster." Donny said without hesitation.

"Same for me!" Abby said, and that was that.

When they left the store Max said, "You folks are welcome anytime. I live up above the shop. You need anything, I'll be here."

Abby kissed his cheek. "Max, you're a treasure. Thanks for everything."

They left the for once speechless Max on the doorstep, still blushing, and climbed into Alex's car.

Alex looked at his watch, it was three p.m. "We have time to visit the Statue of Liberty if you like. You can do the Empire State tomorrow."

He drove off down to Battery Park.

Alex dropped the pair at their hotel later that afternoon, drove downtown and parked. He thought for a few minutes, then took out his cell phone and punched a speed-dial number. He spoke clearly and quietly. "I strongly advise you to leave these two kids alone. They have done nothing here and from my meeting today they are not an easy mark. Also they are now armed. If I had tried to kill them I don't think you would be receiving this call. Do not call me again." He switched off the cell phone and dropped it to the ground. With his heel he smashed the handset to pieces.

Chapter two

The Peugeot cruised west on Route 78 towards Harrisburg. They expected to spend the night there before a long day tomorrow to Akron, Ohio.

"Do you realize that Harrisburg is the capitol of Pennsylvania, and it stands on the Susquehanna River?" Abby was reading from a guide to Pennsylvania as Donny tooled the car along the highway.

"Tell me. Why we are not going to Philadelphia?"

"Because we have limited time and if we are to see all we want to see, we have to bypass some places. Otherwise we won't make it."

"Right, I've got that sorted. But what about the guy following us? Do you think he'll be disappointed?"

Abby looked at him in disbelief. "You have to be joking. Nobody knew when, or where, we are going. We did not know ourselves until we left New York, and we have told nobody, not even our folks."

"So, they have been keeping an eye on us. I don't know how, or why. I do know that the scruffy panel van behind us has followed every move we have made since we left the hotel this morning. It was one of the reasons I called in at Allentown."

"So it wasn't the jail, then?"

"That was the excuse. I just wanted to check and make sure I was not paranoid, if you see what I mean. After all, during the past couple of years we do seem to have attracted a certain amount of attention from people we really did not want to know. I don't think I would have noticed, for a while at least, if we had not been jumped by that bunch of idiots at the motel in West Warwick."

Abby thought for a few minutes. Then she said, "We are going to have to give them a chance sometime. Better to do it on our terms. So let's work out where would be a good place to set up."

They were driving down the William Penn Freeway so when they reached the I -72 south they turned and drove down to Lebanon. At Maple Street, before reaching the town itself, there was a stretch of woodland with a lake in the centre. Here they pulled off the road.

"Trees?" Abby said.

Donny nodded checking the magazine in the Walther as he stepped carefully across to the treeline and vanished.

Abby called softly, "Have you got your comm unit?" Her receiver vibrated for a moment which meant 'yes' in their own code. "Where are you?" she called. I would rather not shoot you by mistake.

Donny appeared for a moment beside a tree. Abby stepped into the cool area beneath the trees where she had been standing.

The panel van appeared around the bend some two hundred and fifty yards down the quiet road. The driver saw the parked car and the vehicle wobbled slightly as he recognized it. Someone obviously told him to pass and stop beyond the location where the car was parked.

Nothing happened for several minutes. Then three men in suits got out of the van. All were armed with Kalashnikov AK47's with the distinctive banana magazine. The road was still quiet as the three men walked along the road, back toward the parked Peugeot.

The man in the lead lifted his weapon and aimed randomly at the woods in front of him and squeezed the trigger. The sound of a pistol shot was lost in the clatter of the sub-machine gun. The man toppled to the ground, dropping his gun to clasp his wounded shoulder, the blood already staining his dark-grey suit.

The other two men opened up with their own weapons, waving the guns back and forth trying to find the concealed pair.

A double crack from the anonymous trees dropped number two and the third looked in horror at his smashed sub-machine gun. He started to reach for his automatic, only to see the Walther in the steady hand of the young man who appeared in front of him. "Don't even think about it!"

He dropped the ruined gun and lifted his hands. "Take your gun out with your left hand, and drop it on the ground."

Abby was checking on the two wounded men. She retrieved their handguns and busied herself attending to their wounds. As she pointed out it was all a bit rough and ready. After all they had asked for it.

"On your knees!" Donny ordered.

Resigned to the idea that he was to be shot, the man obeyed.

"So, who sent you?" The question was unexpected and the man replied without thinking.

"Molotov!" He shut up quickly.

Donny bent over and looked him in the eye. "Now, tell me what this is all about?"

"I don't know nothin'. I just got told to go with the others and do what I am told. Honest. I din' know we was going out to shoot someone until we was already on the road chasing that French car."

Donny looked at Abby with eyebrow raised.

"Use his belt and tie him. By the time he gets free and finds the distributor cap we will be long gone." She walked over to the parked van and opened the rear door. On the floor was a rolled carpet that twitched.

She called Donny over, indicating the carpet.

Donny, having completed tying his man, came over, saw the carpet and grabbed the end, hauling it from the van. It dropped onto the grass with a thud and cry from the person inside.

While Abby covered him, Donny took out his pocket knife and cut the string tied round the carpet roll. Gripping the end he hauled on the carpet, causing the person inside to roll as the carpet opened out fully, depositing a small woman onto the grass verge with a burst of language that sounded rude, even to someone who did not understand New York slang.

She was speaking round a strip of cloth that had been used as a gag. She had managed to move it a certain extent but it was still inhibiting her speech. Her hands had been tied behind her back and her shapely legs tied at the ankles with towelling strips. She had managed to stretch them a little but not sufficiently to allow her to escape.

Abby sliced the ankle-ties then the wrists. The woman herself tore the gag free. There was a small explosion of what sounded like Russian expletives. Then she turned to her rescuers and said in English "And who the hell are you?"

Abby looked at her in amazement.

Donny answered for both of them. "We are the people who have just released you. Who are you?"

The question seemed to wake the woman up to the situation. She looked at the men lying on the ground. "Oh, I'm sorry. I hadn't realized. She looked further. My father will not be happy about this."

"Who is your father?"

"Walter Susskind!" She said it as if they would immediately know who he was. "I am Shirley Susskind."

She looked at Donny and Abby, who were still not impressed, thus showed no reaction to her information whatsoever.

Impatient, Shirley Susskind said. "You must have heard of my father. He is Attorney General of Massachusetts."

"Sorry, we're on holiday from Britain when we got mixed up with this bunch of losers. They seemed to think we would be an easy mark." Donny grinned. "I suppose it was exciting for a while anyway. How did you manage to get rolled up in a rug? It all looked pretty serious to me."

"I suppose I was kidnapped.

Abby said, "You suppose? Don't you know?"

"I was out with friends and I must have had too much to drink." She looked puzzled for a moment. "I don't understand, really. I'm not a drinker, not actually into that sort of thing. I prefer to keep control of things. I can only think I was slipped a Mickey Finn. Who are these guys anyway?"

"As far as I can make out, they are a mixed bunch Russians and an American, presumably Mob, perhaps Mafia. Is there any reason you can think of that would make the Mafia want to kidnap you? Maybe to get control of your father?"

"I really have no idea. My father has his life in the office but he doesn't bring it home. If he is worried, he keeps it to himself or maybe confides in my mother. Either way he doesn't tell me about it."

Donny nudged the captive with his toe, "Any ideas?"

The man shrugged. "I guess it's what you said. They want a hold on the Attorney General for some reason. I think he is known for his attacks on the organization. At least that was what I heard."

"Why, thank you. What's your name?"

The man growled, "Charlie."

Abby said, "So, what are you doing with a bunch of Russian hoods, Charlie?"

"You know—one thing leads to another—and before you know it, you're in over your head. I guess I earned what I've got coming."

"Well, that's up to you and your friends here. We are gone."

"Abby, Shirley! We're leaving."

The women climbed into the Peugeot and Donny took the wheel. He looked at Shirley. "We are headed for Harrisburg. Can we drop you off?"

"I live in Greenwich Village, so if it's not too inconvenient I'll come with you to the Rail Depot. Oh!" She started and opened the door again. "Please, my purse and cell-phone." She leapt out of the car and went over and frisked all three men, retrieving her billfold with her credit cards and a wad of notes from one of the wounded men. Then she ran to the van and found her purse and phone in the glove-box.

Back in the car, she grinned and waved a fistful of cash. "Dinner is on the Mafia."

Donny shrugged, "Why not?"

Abby thought of the collection of additional guns in the trunk of the car. With a sigh she thought, *Here we go again!*

On the drive down to Harrisburg, Shirley confided that she was still studying at Columbia for her degree in Sociology. She had considered taking Law to follow her father in his career but had been persuaded to opt for Social studies instead. Apparently it was the coming thing in an increasingly popular welfare culture currently sweeping the United States.

"What the hell. I can switch to law if it seems the thing to do next semester. So you say you are both at Brunel University? Where the hell is that? I have heard of Oxford and Cambridge, but Brunel?"

"It's in a place called Uxbridge, in Middlesex, West of London."

"We have a place called Uxbridge here near Worcester, now you mention it, so what do you study?"

"We are both Law students. Donny's father is a solicitor, an attorney, in Christchurch on the south coast of England."

"What brought you to the US of A, this bright and sunny day?"

"We are enjoying a gap year. Over the past six months we have travelled in Europe, so when we were offered the opportunity to do an all-expense-paid, cross-country cruise across America, we took it."

Abby asked "Where were you when they kidnapped you?"

"I was visiting friends at home in Boston. We went out for a few laughs and a drink at one of the clubs. I got separated from them in the crowd and I got a soft drink from the bar. Next thing I know I'm being rolled out in a carpet."

"I guess I was going somewhere for delivery to the next place down the line, when my guys were diverted to deal with you two. Now it's your turn. Why in hell would the Mafia here be interested in two visiting law students from England?"

Donny looked at Abby and shrugged.

Abby said. "It's a long story. We'll tell you over that dinner you promised, okay?"

"Deal!" Shirley laughed. "I'll hold you to that."

They pulled into the Holiday Inn parking lot on the outskirts of the city, where they decided to take a break and maybe spend the night. At

Shirley's request they took a family room as she was more shaken than she had admitted.

In the restaurant Abby gave Shirley the shortened version of her life since meeting Donny, including the story of the previous six months. Even in her mind that period was the most traumatic. When she finished she sat back and carried on eating.

Shirley looked at Donny. "Is she for real?" She asked incredulously, "the shooting, the Spetnatz, the threats."

Donny smiled, nodded, and said with a shrug, "Life has been interesting ever since our first crossing to France together; seemed like just one thing after another."

"Wow, and I'm upset by a little kidnapping. I am glad you guys are on my side."

In their room they took turns with the bathroom, Abby supplied spare things for Shirley. They bought toiletries to add to those supplied by the hotel, and all three crashed out, grateful for the soft beds and anonymity of the hotel room.

***

Donny wakened first and remembering that they were not alone, dived into the bathroom to wash and shave before the others started stirring.

He went down to the car, drove to the nearest gas station where he fuelled, and restocked the small cooler with soft drinks.

Back at the hotel he went into the dining room and collected breakfast. He was still finishing his eggs and bacon when the two women joined him.

"You were away early this morning." Abby said.

"I wanted to get the car fuelled and ready for a quick getaway this morning. I don't like the idea of the bunch who tried to ambush us having another chance too soon."

The girls got their breakfasts and came back to join him.

"What do you want to do today, Shirley?" Abby asked.

"I suppose I ought to contact my dad and see what he has to say, but I would really feel safer back in New York with the college crowd."

"Well, we can drop you off, or you can catch the bus or train from here." Donny produced the timetables for both that he had found in the reception of the hotel.

"Oh, oh. Ladies we may have a problem." Donny spoke quietly and bent his head. The room was more crowded now and it seemed that the two men who had just walked in had not yet seen them. "Yul Brunner has just walked in," he muttered.

Puzzled, Shirley said, "Yul Brunner?"

"I'll explain later," Donny said. "Abby, make for the restroom. Shirley, stay low and join the group that is just leaving. We'll meet at the car outside." He passed the keys to Abby. "Go now." As the two girls departed in different directions he went out the lobby and got into the elevator. At the first floor he stopped and pressed the next three buttons, before leaving the car.

In the other car, he made his way to the basement garage and crouched down to the floor. He allowed the doors to open then—as they closed—he rolled out, after pressing the button for the ground floor. Hidden behind a black Galaxy, he waited and listened.

His patience was rewarded he heard a shoe scrape and a voice murmured about three cars away. He drew the gun from his belt and pushed off the safety. Then he crawled round until he could see who was waiting.

A tall man in jeans and plaid shirt was leaning against a pick-up truck. The cowboy boots and broad-brimmed hat did not disguise the fact that the only plains this man would have ridden crossed were not in America. His companion was wearing combat pants and a tee shirt emblazoned with a Rolling Stones logo. His cropped hair and Slavic look reminded him of the Spet-natz he had encountered in France.

Donny moved carefully along the row of cars until he was close to the garage entrance.

A car started up at the other end of the ga-rage as a guest started out. Guessing the two watchers would be distracted and with the gun down by his side, Donny walked out of the entry.

He had left the car outside in the open park-ing area. The two girls were just getting in as he joined them, slipping his gun away as he did.

They left the hotel without a tail and made off to the train station, where Shirley booked her seat to New York. Abby suggested that she speak to her father and tell him what was hap-pening.

The phone call was awkward. The two Brit-ons heard her say "But, Dad, they weren't stu-dents playing pranks. For Pete's sake they shot at my friends, and two of then finished up wounded." There was silence, then, "Lebanon. Yes, Lebanon." more silence. Then. "They didn't kill them. When we left there were two with wounds and one unwounded but tied up with his belt." Silence. Then, "The fact that it's your daughter telling you means nothing, does it? Damn you! No wonder Mother left you. It's lucky my friends were there to help me. If it was up to you I would probably be dead or raped rotten by now." She slammed the phone down and turned to Donny and Abby. "Sorry, guys. It would be best if you faded out at this point. The three men you rescued me from, are now two dead, one missing. The van's gone and they are looking for a foreign car with three or four people in it. I guess my dad will have the local police here pretty quickly. He doesn't believe me."

She opened the door. "Get going fast, while you still have time. I will tell them that you dropped me off and headed south for Florida." She kissed them both hurriedly and thanked them. They left the area heading west. Donny said "Someone searched our luggage."

"Who do you think?"

"It had to be Shirley."

Abby sighed, "I guess so." She lifted her handbag. "She missed out on this, though."

They spent that night in Altoona.

***

Two days later Abby was driving toward Akron when Donny, said "I think we have company."

Abby drove on. "Let's check it out!" She took the next right off the highway signposted Ashtabula, according to the map, a place on the shores of Lake Erie.

They reached the lakeside city just over one hour later.

"I haven't seen them since we turned off Highway 76 at Youngtown. I think maybe we lost them. I am worried how they managed to pick us up so quickly. Do you have Shirley's number?"

Abby pulled over into the Wal-Mart car park. "I'll call her." She tapped out the number from a note she had made at the apartment. There was no answer. "I don't like this at all. I keep feeling we are missing something. Donny, do you think that they could have bugged the car?"

"No, I don't think they've had the opportunity. But I do think they might be able to trace the phone."

"But I got this phone here. It's just a pay-as-you-go throwaway. You know, you were there when I bought it."

"So was Alex. In fact, if I recall, he chose it for you."

"But why would the FBI want to keep tabs on us? All we have done is protect ourselves."

"Assuming it is the FBI? I think it's time we had a chat with Jonathon."

Donny got out and walked round to the trunk of the car and opened his suitcase. He retrieved the laptop-sized case and returned to his seat in the car. Checking the time, he opened the case and extended the aerial attached to the instrument within. He pressed two buttons, causing a red light to come on. He then extracted a connecting cable that he plugged into the car power socket. A green light appeared and an LED screen lit up with a list of touch options. He pressed the top icon. The sound of dialling followed confirming the connection and the fact that the speakerphone was active.

"Hullo, you two. How are you enjoying America?" The voice of Jonathon Glynn came loud and clear.

"Jonathon, do you know an Alex Randall?" Donny asked directly.

The reply came almost immediately, the short delay between comments a penalty of long-range sound communication. "Short, slightly overweight, wears Armani suits, always charcoal grey. 'Friar Tuck' hairstyle and chews gum 24/7."

Donny replied "Six foot, full head of sandy hair, clean-shaven, blue eyes and Hollywood teeth. Sharp dresser, East Coast accent."

"No! Sounds like a ringer. How did you meet, and why am I worrying?"

Abby explained and mentioned the cell phone.

Jonathon said, "Dump it on another truck or car, or trash it. Remember if you trash it they will know they have been found out."

They explained about the other events and Yul Brunner, Shirley Susskind and their present position.

While they were speaking Jonathon was working his computer.

"The Shirley Susskind you describe does not exist. Her so-called father, the Attorney General of Massachusetts is seventy–two and his daughter Shirley is fifty years old and lives in Hawaii with her husband who is a Judge in the Supreme Court there. My suggestion is arm yourselves and start watching your back a little more carefully. This is a number you can call if you need help." He reeled off a number that Donny wrote down and rang off.

The two youngsters looked at each other. Donny put the phone away, and looked around the car park area. While he watched, a delivery truck pulled into the commercial area at the side of the building. "I'm just off to see where to send that cell phone." He held his hand out and was passed the suspect phone. "Why don't you buy another, in fact make it two, and a two way communication system, to keep in touch."

Abby went into the huge market while Donny went prospecting around the side of the building to the delivery area.

The cell phone was well on its way to Niagara Falls by the time Donny located Abby in Wal-Mart.

Chapter three

The Peugeot made the journey to Akron effortlessly, the deceptively quiet engine a murmur in the background of the music from the radio. Neither of the couple was really feeling like talking as both were absorbed by their own thoughts. For Donny there was the worry that the people they had encountered already were still on their tail; perhaps using an alternative tracker, not the cell phone at all.

For Abby it was something else, she was puzzled over the matter of the girl who called herself Shirley Susskind. She was trying to work out why she had been rolled up in the carpet. All the signs were that she had been in fact kidnapped. *But if she wasn't Shirley Susskind, why would anyone kidnap her? Unless there was some advantage to be gained there was no reason to snatch someone. Judging by the gag and the bindings it could not have been comfortable wrapped up the way she was. Donny was pretty sure that the man he questioned had not known about the girl, so the Russians took her before they were diverted to deal with us. There was the obvious of course; she was very pretty and sexy in her own way. But no: the carpet, the tying up and gagging, it was all too planned for some spontaneous sexual escapade, even if it did include rape and possible murder.*

It felt like a kidnap to put pressure on someone or revenge perhaps, and if it wasn't the Attorney General, then who?

Donny interrupted her train of thought at that time, "This is Akron now. I don't know how you feel but to me it's early still and I would like to carry on for a while, how about it? Stop or go on?"

The couple had been close for nearly three years now and there was a rapport between them that often resulted in finishing each other's sentences, and even thinking the same thoughts. Abby smiled and looked across at Donny. "You know you love driving, you never want to stop. This time I agree with you. Let's keep going until you really want to stop. I would like to explore Chicago, though."

They both burst out laughing at the thought of reaching Chicago, approximately 400 miles away. After all it was already three-thirty in the afternoon.

They finally stopped at Findlay, Ohio, at a crossroad motel. They parked, checked in, and went to the Cracker Barrel Store next door, still open, and happily, serving food. After they ate they strolled around the retail area, before returning to their room and collapsing on the bed, tired after the long day.

The following morning they drove to Dearborn for a planned visit the Henry Ford Museum.

The weather was fine so they elected to take the rail tour of the park that was the external part of the Museum.

Donny's cell phone rang. He was still using his British phone. It was one that could be used internationally. The number displayed was the number Jonathon had given them for a local contact, so he answered it. "Hi. Who is this?"

"My name is Charlie Herrick, and I am a friend of Jonathon. You are Donny, right?"

"Yes !"

"You have company! Your car is being watched as I speak. The watchers are not nice people. They are sitting in a blue Chevy with a white stripe, in the car park opposite your Peugeot. They have not touched it, but I guess the car must be bugged already otherwise they would not be here. I will delay their departure but I suggest you lose the car and get something else less conspicuous. I am on my own. I cannot hold them back for long. So once you reach the car park, call and I will see what I can do. Okay?"

"Sounds good to me, but we may be able to help delay them."

"Please leave it to me. Concentrate on getting away fast!"

The man rang off. They looked at each other, Donny shrugged.

Abby said, "I'm getting fed up with all this. I'll leave it this time; but if they catch up again, I vote we do something about it ourselves."

Donny looked at her, then leaned forward and kissed her. "Absolutely. I agree! Now let's go, I think it's time to leave."

They walked back to the Exhibition building. Donny called Charlie "We are coming out now." They strolled out through the doors and made for the car.

"That must be them." Donny indicated a car parked opposite theirs, the white stripe quite obvious against the almost black background. They could not distinguish the occupants; the sun glinting off the angled windshield made it impossible to see through.

As they entered their car, the vehicle opposite started up. Donny drove out and the other car started to follow. It then stopped abruptly, rocking on its springs; the starter whirred as they tried to restart the car. The last Donny saw of it was of the door opening and a man getting out.

They set out for Chicago then and there. On the way they stopped beside one of the many river crossings where, timing things as gaps appeared in the traffic, they dumped the assembled armoury of captured weapons.

At Gary they left the car with the rental company and boarded the bus for the city. They dropped off at Oak Lawn and found a boarding house where they were taken in hand by the owner, a British lady who had married a GI at the end of the war and moved to Chicago with him. Now a widow for several years, Julia Bellamy still retained a strong affection for all things British and Donny and Abby benefitted accordingly.

From their room overlooking the lake, the curve of shoreline of the city was visible. The skyline of buildings familiar through TV programs and movies they had both been brought up on.

With directions from their hostess, they took the green-line train into the City, where they roamed the streets for the day. They ate at the Billy Goat Tavern because Donny had been told about it by his father. He had been to Chicago when he was younger. On advice they took a tour bus that roamed the loop and pointed out the main historic sites of the center of the city.

For Donny it was enough and on the train back to Oak Lawn he took Abby's hand and looked into her eyes. "Abby, I miss the sea. I don't miss the big city. How about we hire a boat and just chill for a few days?"

She looked at him, then leaned forward and kissed him, causing a few amused looks from the other passengers. "Why not?" she said. "My feet are killing me. Tomorrow we'll find a boat and cruise north for a few days, away from it all."

Donny pulled her close, enjoying the scent of her skin, and the feel of her body warm and yielding against him. "I do love you, Abby Marshall," he whispered in her ear.

"I love you too, Donny Weston." She whispered back and kissed his ear before they separated settled back on their seats.

Mrs. Bellamy knew someone. It was the following morning and the pick-up that came to the house was driven by a friendly young man named George, who hugged Mrs Bellamy and called her 'aunty'. He worked for the local boat rental company at the marina on the lakeshore.

His boss was a big man. "Call me Pete," he said. "Everybody does. You're looking for a boat to hire? Sail? Motor-boat? Day-boat, or cruiser?

"Sail cruise," Donny said quickly. "We are both qualified sea sailors, certified in navigation and boat handling. We have a 40-ft ketch at home.

Pete looked at the pair. "My sister vouches for you. Let's take an hour on the 'Bitch'. After that, we'll see how to go. Okay?"

Both young people nodded, though neither realized what he was talking about when he referred to the 'Bitch'.

It turned out to be a twenty-one foot deep keel, Dragon-class day-boat, with a full suite of sails.

Fitted out with floatation gear, the three boarded the 'Bitch' from a dinghy. Pete sat amidships and left them to it.

Both were happy to be back on the water and they fell into routine immediately. The foresail was unrolled and the main sail was raised in minutes. While Abby released the mooring, Donny sailed the slim sailor out of the marina area with cool efficiency.

Abby called, "We have a genoa and a spinnaker here, if you like?"

"Let's start with the jenny, and try the spinnaker later. We'll feel the winds first, I think."

Pete nodded approvingly, though neither of the others noticed, since both were concentrating on the serious business of sailing the boat.

When they returned to the mooring Pete stepped ashore and waved at the assortment of sailing cruisers in their slots in the marina. "Take your choice" he said. None is hired for the next three weeks. There will be no extra charge whichever you choose. All are fuelled and all have a tender. There will be a week's basic food in the fridge and freezer. The cooler is topped up with soft drinks and beer. Power is on from the shore, so unplug before you sail and switch to engine and generator power when you sail off.

Donny looked at Abby and they strolled off down the row of boats. They ranged from a sixty-foot schooner to a thirty-foot, four-berth sloop. They looked through most of the boats there but settled for the sloop. They returned to Mrs Bellamy and packed two small cases from their luggage. Mrs Bellamy put a big basket of her home-made bread and several other packed items in the pick-up for them to take with them.

They sailed at midday, and had their first meal aboard while still battling with the gusty winds channelled by the tall buildings on the shore.

***

The next five days passed quietly and, for the two young people not having to bother with others, a welcome change to the last two weeks of looking over their shoulders.

Eventfully they had to return the boat and resume their cross-country trip. The return to civilization meant an encounter with a string of unanswered messages and emails, as the twenty-first century intruded with a bang. The new rental was a Galaxy, and though it provided plenty of room for luggage and themselves, it was not the beloved Peugeot.

Rather than travel along the major roads all the time, they decided to take the lesser roads and make it more difficult for any trackers to keep in touch. It unfortunately had disadvantages as well. After only one day they turned off the road they were following in the region of Grand Rapids, following signs to Country Hotel. It was dark by the time they reached the place which seemed to be close to a village, judging by the scatter of lights down the slope below the Hotel. Donny parked the Galaxy while Abby went in to register.

He looked at the dark area around the hotel, shrugged and slipped the Walther into his belt behind his back, picked up the two cases and walked into the hotel.

There was a bar off to the right and the reception desk on the left. Several people were using the bar. Abby was bending over the reception desk, signing in. A man came out of the bar, bottle in hand. He was big and unshaven and Donny could see immediately he was trouble. The man was looking at Abby, smiling and swaying slightly.

Donny walked past him as Abby turned holding the room key in her hand. "Come on, slowpoke," she called. "Bath time!"

The big man leered at her. "Sounds good," he said. "I'll bring the beer."

Abby turned and looked at him. "In your dreams, buster." And set off walking to the stairs.

Another man appeared by the stairs, from a corridor with the restrooms sign. He stood blocking the way up the stairs.

The hotel receptionist called out, "Get out of the way, Linus. Just let the lady through."

"Aw, Charlie. There ain't no fun round here anymore. Would you like to dance, lady?" he reached out to grab Abby and regretted it. She said, "We haven't been introduced," then stepping aside, kicked his shin with her booted foot.

Linus hopped about swearing, holding his bruised leg. Donny and Abby went upstairs while the two drunks consoled each other.

In their room Donny looked at the lock on the door. He placed a chair under the doorknob. "That should do it, for now.

Abby looked at him defiantly. "What?" she said.

"This is not a good place to make enemies," he said mildly.

"I thought I was very restrained," Abby said. "He stank."

Donny took the Walther from its place and sat on the bed. "This is not England," he said. "And I am not altogether happy about our friend down below."

When they went down to eat the men were gone. The manager of the hotel appeared and apologised for the incident.

When he left them, Abby said with a smile, "I trust the manager even less than Linus. He gives me the creeps!"

"I agree, but we're here now and there doesn't seem to be much choice in this area. We have to make the best of it, I'm afraid."

The night passed without incident and they left the following morning, heading back the several miles to the highway.

The ambush was on a bend, and there were no other vehicles in sight. The two pick-up trucks were parked across the road effectively blocking the way past.

Donny was driving and he drew up well back from the vehicles. Two men appeared from the trees on the left of the road and a third from the right. All carried shotguns, casually not really pointed at anyone, but ready to if needed. Abby slid her Walther PPK from beneath her seat and checked that the magazine was loaded, the click as it slotted home was only audible in the car. Donny opened the car door and stepped out; his gun was hidden but ready for use.

"Would you mind moving your truck?" he called.

Linus stepped into view from behind the right-hand pick-up.

The older man of the four called to Linus, "Is that the pussytail you was talking about last night, Linus? Why, she ain't big enough to look after all four of us. Yore sassy niece has more on her, than that one."

Donny spoke again his voice harder. "Time to shift that pick-up. I don't want to waste any more time here."

The older man turned on him lifting the shotgun but without touching the trigger. "You lookie here, sonny. This gun says that I can say and do what I damn well please. Understand!"

Donny looked at him for a few moments. Then he said slowly and carefully, "I do not wish to hurt you so I will give you one more chance to get your trucks out of the way."

Behind him Abby stepped down from the Galaxy. Her gun out of sight but ready also. Donny heard her and set himself for the action that was surely going to happen.

Linus stepped forward with a grin. "Shoot the kid, Daddy. I'll bring the girl and we can have some fun before we bury her."

The older man lifted the shotgun. Abby shot him. His gun fell to the ground and he looked at his arms in disbelief. The bullet had passed through both forearms. And his blood was puddling in the dust. The other armed men both swung up their own guns but Donny's first shot took the near man in the shoulder, his second hit the other man in the leg and he collapsed to the ground with a shout. "I'm hit. I'm hit."

Linus pulled out a big revolver and eared back the hammer aiming at Abby. "You bitch!" He screamed. "You shot my daddy."

Abby dropped to the ground and Linus's shot missed. Donny got to him while he was still pulling back the hammer for another try. Donny knocked the gun out of his hand. It went off as it hit the ground though the bullet did not hit anyone. Linus swung on Donny, but before he could set himself Abby was facing him, no gun, and a smile on her face. "You want me. I'm here."

The man lunged forward and stopped as his nose spouted blood. "Hey," he cried. "That hurt!" The booted foot that caught him on the side of his head hurt also, and, knocked off balance, he finished on his hands and knees in the dust. He shook his head and looked at the slim girl in front of him: her long legs, neat miniskirt and short jacket, serious pretty face with hair back in a ponytail. He lurched to his feet and wary of the boots started to circle round looking for an opening. He just needed to get his hands on her and it would all be over.

He lunged forward suddenly and caught her short jacket, ripping it back exposing her white blouse. She turned within his arms and her elbow slammed into his midriff. His face turned red and he tried to get air into his suddenly starved lungs. The elbow was followed by an upper cut that rattled his teeth. The top of her forehead hit his battered nose and it was all over. Linus collapsed to the ground wheezing gasping for breath and wondering which way was up.

Donny was moving one of the pick-ups out of the way. The three wounded men were not interested in anything but the task of stemming their blood and cursing.

Abby looked ruefully at her designer jacket, the tear was across the front panel. She took it off and removed her cards from the small concealed pocket. Walking over to Linus she dropped the jacket beside him, and walked over to the Galaxy. She drove past the remaining pick-up and Donny jumped out of the other vehicle and joined her. They reached the highway ten minutes later and turned west.

They made good time approaching Des Moines, Iowa, in the early afternoon. It was there they discovered that they were still being followed.

Chapter four

The black Crown Victoria drew up alongside their parked car. Donny was leaning on the door as the driver got out. He was not at all surprised when the man held up his FBI identification wallet. It named him as Special Agent Peter Harris.

"Donny and Abby, I presume?" He was as tall as Donny but heavier built, wearing a grey suit that was out of place in the circumstances.

"We are going in for coffee and something to eat. Join us!" Donny was feeling pretty pissed at the attention they were attracting, one way and another.

The three people entered the diner and sat at a table. They accepted the offered coffee and placed their orders for food. When they were alone once more, Donny turned to the FBI man for some sort of explanation.

"I got this message. Contact you two pass on the message. Then make myself scarce. Okay?"

"So, pass on the message."

"This guy, Molotov, was Spetnatz. He was cousin to Adam Markov who runs a local version

of the Mafia in New York. You actually killed
his cousin in some place in France. The word
was received here without a ripple; until some
nosey guy pointed out that you two were actually
here in the USA. He thinks this maybe has made
it a matter of face. You both went on to the hit
list, and you should really consider returning to
UK by the first flight. But you won't. So keep
your eyes open and your powder dry. The message came from some guy called Jonathon
Glynn, MI6."

The waitress reappeared and served their
food and all conversation finished while they ate.

Peter Harris was facing the window directly.
Both Donny and Abby were sitting each side of
him beside the window.

Abby noticed Peter's face go pale and his
gaze fixed on something out of her line of sight.
She reached her foot out and kicked Donny,
nodding at Peter.

"What is it, Peter?" Donny asked. "Someone
you know?"

Peter said quietly, "Don't make any sudden
moves. Just casually get up and go to the rest
rooms, both of you."

"Why?" Abby asked.

"Because outside beside your car is one of
the biggest men in the Russian Mafia all the way

from Chicago. By biggest I mean largest. He is very nasty and virtually unstoppable. Now go!"

The two young people looked at each other and both shook their heads in unison. "No, I don't think so," Donny said. "If we are going to get any peace on this holiday, we have to end things now." Reaching behind him he pulled out the Walther and, under the cover of the table, checked the magazine and cocked the weapon, the click of Abby's gun sounding in turn almost immediately.

Peter looked at them incredulously. "What do you think you are doing?"

"Why? Preparing to defend ourselves," Donny said innocently. "Isn't that written into the Constitution?"

"But there are five of them out there, including Mad Ivan. And they haven't seen you yet. You can still get away."

"And have them sneak up on us when we aren't prepared. No, thank you. Now is as good a time as any. Ready?" Donny looked at Abby. She nodded and they both rose from their seats and made for the door.

With a resigned shrug, the big FBI man rose to his feet. Drawing his Glock automatic, he racked a round into the chamber and walked over to join them.

Outside the five men had split up, walking up and down the street, looking in the shops and cafes as they went. Mad Ivan turned toward the diner as the three people came out; guns in hand hanging down at their sides.

Whether he noticed the guns or not, he ignored them. "They are here." He shouted the others down the street and passing pedestrians turned to see what was happening. When the four others produced guns the other people using the sidewalks scattered into the buildings either side of the street, leaving the Russians and their targets to their fate.

Donny didn't hesitate. Ivan produced a big automatic and was firing before the gun was level. Donny kept cool and shot him in the chest. The impact of his shot stopped the Russian in his tracks. His vest stopped the bullet penetrating, but though he staggered, he did not fall. He lifted the big gun once more but died before the gun was level. Donny made no mistake, his second shot created a third eye in the Russian's forehead and he dropped like a stone.

The others had concentrated on the four men who accompanied Mad Ivan. All started shooting from wherever they were at the time. Bullets flew everywhere. There was a mini Uzi that drained its magazine everywhere but at the three facing them. Peter had adopted the stance favored by US law enforcement agencies; feet apart, both hands gripping the Glock firmly in front of him. Abby stood sideways, as if in an old-fashioned duel, gun in her right hand, casually lining up her arm with the target and shooting twice at each target. Donny had swung round to Peter's side and his next shot took one of the Russians in the leg, dropping him to the ground screaming. Peter's other target was missing a face where the two bullets had impacted side by side.

It was all over in three minutes, four dead and one screaming with a shattered shin. Donny approached the wounded man cautiously but he was not going to offer any trouble, so Donny kicked away his weapon and checked the other body.

Peter did the check on the others. There was another survivor, unconscious from a bullet graze, with broken ribs from the impact of a bullet to his ill-fitting Kevlar vest.

The wail of sirens heralded the arrival of the local police.

Donny and Abby were seated in their car when first Police car arrived. Peter stood with hands raised and his badge displayed. Luckily, he was recognized by one of the policemen who holstered his gun and with hands on hips swore and said, "What the hell happened here?"

"These guys came out of nowhere looking for someone. They thought they had found them and started shooting." Peter looked at the men innocently.

The second cop said, "You know this guy, Harry?"

"Yeah, he's the local FBI guy. He comes and lectures us on the latest wanted list. He's okay."

The second cop put his gun away. "He had help!" He observed.

"Yeah." Peter said, "But I can't tell you about it. I'll need to talk to your Captain."

The ambulance arrived and the medics started to go to work on the wounded men.

Peter said, "I'll leave this mess for you guys to clear up and take my friends to the station with me to see the Captain, will that be okay?"

Harry waved to him. "Go see the Captain, then. Jesus, you don't piss about when you're attacked do you!"

Peter came over to Donny and Abby and climbed into the back seat.

Donny said, "What about their car?"

"Damn, I must be slipping. Let's take a look before we go." He opened the door and got out followed by the two young people and walked over to the car that the Russians had used.

In the trunk, the survivor of the last attack on Donny and Abby was lying there shivering. His wound had been exposed, the dressing ripped off and someone had been carving pieces of flesh from the bloody mess. He was still alive.

Abby turned away sick at the sight of the brutalized man. Peter called the medics over. Harry came with them and gagged at the sight. They removed the man and took him to the ambulance for transport to hospital. The rest of the car produced gum wrappers and a carton that had contained doughnuts. The ashtrays were full of cigarette butts. However, under the front seat there was a torn piece of paper. It was headed with the crest of the United States Government.

There was no addressee, that part was torn off, but there was enough of the text left to identify the broadly expressed itinerary of ... estern and ...by Marshall. The tears had left partial words only.

Peter looked at the paper in dismay.

Donny asked, "Can you tell which department sent it?"

"Not really," Peter said. "The headings are all the same with the department added on the left below the Eagle. With it torn off as it is, the department name has been removed. We cannot even narrow it down to a typewriter as we did in the past. This is generated on a computer.

"It does explain how the opposition seem to be able to get on our trail so easily," Abby said. "I think we should check out our car before we leave here, just in case they stuck a tracer on it."

At Police Headquarters they gave their statements under the close supervision of Peter Harris. They were then released to continue their trip without interference. They checked over the car for bugs, said goodbye to Peter Harris, and set out for Denver as scheduled.

Just the other side of the airport Donny turned south for Kansas City, "Just to make things a little more awkward for them if they pick us up," was the way he put it.

They stayed overnight at a motel on a road junction and started early the following morning, had breakfast in Kansas City and turned west towards Denver.

"Have you thought about getting married at all?" Donny asked Abby.

"What brought that on?" Abby looked at him sharply.

"Well, I just wondered if you had. That's all." He shrugged as if it was just an idle thought.

"Of course I have, you daft bugger. I would not be here now if it hadn't crossed my mind.

But before you get too excited, I think we are both too young to consider that. After all, how could you afford to keep me while we are still at University, unless you are leaving to go to work? I certainly have no intention of leaving until I've got my degree."

"Nor will I, and I'm not daft, I was just trying to look ahead a little. That's all."

Abby looked at him suspiciously. You're not going to spring a proposal on me when I am not looking, I hope?"

"As I just said, I have no intention of proposing to you at present. I believe I have made it quite clear that I will when I think the time is right. Meanwhile, I agree with you. We are both too young at the moment." They let the matter rest at that point and started to discuss the attacks made by the Russians since they arrived in America.

"Personally, I cannot believe they would go to all this trouble over some imagined insult to some European's dignity. There must be something that we are missing, something that is worth a lot of trouble." Donny slumped into thoughtful mode.

"Or perhaps they just think we know, or have, something they want." Abby, equally reflective, was considering all they had been involved with over the past few months and was equally mystified. "I have absolutely no idea why we should be targeted in this way. They have lost several men killed and injured to our certain knowledge. While I am aware they regard life as cheap, this has been a bloody ridiculous waste for whatever they are after, unless it is very important or very valuable."

As they progressed generally westward, both spent time wondering about the reason for the attacks.

The helicopter came out of the blue. It roared past the car at low level and rose ahead, turning as it completed the climb. It hovered for a minute or two as the side door slid open. A man appeared in harness carrying a long-barrelled weapon. The figure lined up the weapon with the approaching car, and fired.

Donny, who was driving, floored the accelerator and the car leapt forward. The missile fired from the helicopter missed the car by yards, ploughing a deep furrow and finally blowing a hole in the road surface.

The shooter handed the missile launcher back to someone within the helicopter, and accepted another weapon. The helicopter swung, accelerated to overtake the car and, once again, positioned itself to allow the shooter to aim and fire.

"This is getting tricky," Donny said. "There is only so much I can do to avoid him. Keep your eyes open for some sort of cover."

Abby was cocking her automatic and, as Donny was speaking, leaned out of the car window and she flipped the gun up and fired in one movement. Three sets of two fired in swift succession.

The door-anchored shooter sagged in the harness. The weapon he was holding fell to the ground below.

"Gotcha!" Abby said with quiet satisfaction, reloading her automatic with a fresh magazine.

Donny said, "Lucky! Not the sort of thing you could anticipate."

"Look out!" Abby called jamming her foot on his and causing the car to leap forward once more.

The body of the dead man fell into the road, to one side of the racing car. Apart from the color of his skin glimpsed on passing, neither could say they knew the man. After the impact with the tarmac it would have been difficult for anyone to recognize him.

His employers were obviously not concerned with him. He was of no further use to them dead.

The helicopter had swooped over the hills to the south, so Donny really put his foot down and made distance across the open countryside to the small town of Oakley, Kansas.

There they stopped at a diner in the main street to feed and freshen up.

As they were eating Abby suggested, "How about we keep going tonight and make Denver by morning?" We can take turns driving and sleeping."

Donny looked at her seriously. "If you are up to it, sure. But I think I'll add to our armory before we travel on. I noticed a gun shop as we drove into town. Let's call in there before we travel on."

Abby reached across and rubbed his shoulder. "You got that gleam in your eye when we passed through Abilene. I have the feeling that you want more than a holstered six gun when we travel on."

"Betcha life, I do. I don't think they will run to an H&K smg, but perhaps a Winchester or at least a pump shotgun. With a rifle, when that helicopter appeared, we could have picked him off immediately. As it was your lucky shot was all that saved us."

He concentrated on his food for the next few minutes.

"No ideas why, or who? Apart from the comments about the Russians that is. After all it had to cost money to keep up the chase the way they have."

"All I can think is that there is something we're missing, something important. Perhaps simple in our eyes but important to someone else. Next time we stop over, maybe in Denver, we will have to go through everything we have with us, in detail."

Abby looked at Donny sharply, "Do you think we are carrying something we are not aware of?"

"Could be, I don't know. I am just trying to cover all the bases."

The moon turned the landscape to silver, the rising hills ahead showing sharp black shadows against the highlighted ridges and cols. Abby drove, deep in thought, worried a little over the way trouble seemed to dog their footsteps. It seemed that ever since she had got together with Donny they had been either defending them-selves, or attacking people who were trying to harm them. She had to admit that the first inci-dent had been none of Donny's doing. The at-tempt to smuggle things in the boat could not have been done without the assistance of the un-fortunate Peter Davey. The crude attempt to murder them both by Peter had been almost laughable in contrast with the sophisticated attempts since. It would have been no less lethal had it succeeded.

She thought of the man who had dropped from the helicopter and shivered. She had shot him, probably, as Donny suggested a pure fluke. If she had not, the chances were that they would both have died from the missile the man was firing. It was still a burden to carry, whatever. The man was still dead.

The road ahead was wide and empty with just the occasional semi-trailer to pass or looming up and rushing past in the opposite direction. Abby enjoyed her session at the wheel and allowed Donny to sleep on well past the agreed changeover time. When she eventually woke him and he took over, he told her off for not wakening him at the agreed time. Abby smiled shrugged and curled up and went to sleep the picture of the moonlit landscape still firmly etched in her mind.

They rolled into Denver in the morning in time to get caught up in the morning rush hour. Donny caught sight of a Holiday Inn sign and took the off-ramp from the highway and parked thankfully in the hotel car park.

Donny nudged Abby's sleeping form. "Wake up, sleepy. Give me a hand with the bags."

The pair checked in and dumped their bags in their room and promptly collapsed on the bed.

It was the persistent ringing of his cell phone that woke Donny two hours later. He groaned and looked at the caller name. Jonathon!

"Hullo, Jonathon. What gets you up at this ungodly hour?"

"Ungodly, its 3.00 o'clock in the afternoon here, you should have been up for a couple of hours at least."

Donny looked blearily at his phone. It was 09.31 according to the satellite currently supplying its signal, "What's happening, Jonathon?" Donny asked.

"I was hoping you would tell me. I have reports of dead men on the highway. Backwoods gunfights and helicopters buzzing the traffic on the highway west."

"Whatever or whoever seems to have the idea we are worth pursuing for some reason. Neither Abby nor I have the faintest idea what, or who, they are after. We just seem to be a target. What about you? Do you have any ideas?"

"Sorry, Donny. All I can think of is that the Russians may have marked you for a target. But I can't even think why they should. Perhaps they slipped something into your luggage and they are trying to recover it. I would take a look through your gear and see if there is anything there that you don't remember packing. I should also look for a tracer."

"We had thought of that and we will be going through everything later today."

"If you find you need help, give me a shout. I'll see what I can do. Give my love to Abby and good luck!" Jonathon rang off.

Donny looked at his watch again. Outside it was broad daylight with the sunlight making hard shadows on the face of the walls across the street. The air conditioning was humming quietly keeping the temperature even. The altitude made breathing just a little more difficult. Now, even though he was thoroughly awake, he was tempted to stay in bed. He resisted the urge, rolled out of bed and wandered through to the bathroom, carefully closing the door so as not to awaken Abby.

He was in the shower when he felt the waft of cool air across his back followed by the touch of cool hands slipping round him and grabbing the soap.

After the excitement of the shower the search of their baggage and personal possessions was almost an anti-climax. It was saved from a complete waste of time by the fact that they found something that should not have been there.

Chapter five

In New York things were happening. The offices of the consortium were located in an otherwise anonymous building in Wall Street. It was just another skyscraper full of office suites occupied by bankers, brokers and money-movers of that ilk.

Addison Berkley Inc. was one of the many private banks that specialize in the discreet movement of money throughout the banking world. The eponymous founder had reached an age where money had become just a commodity, so personally rich that he never bothered carrying any. Mundane matters of that sort were left to employees who were paid to perform on his behalf.

His actual participation in the day to day business of the company had long since ceased. That had been placed in the hands of a highly recommended broker who had been head-hunted from one of the most prestigious brokerages in Wall Street.

Charles Regret looked the part. His carefully tended, fair hair not quite perfect, the thousand dollar suits just slightly more casual than the earlier generation of brokers would have approved.

This morning Charles was looking a little less collected than normal. In fact. he was concerned to the point where he considered the possibility of a moonlight departure to points unknown, a prospect he discarded almost as swiftly as it occurred. The people he would be trying to avoid had demonstrated their skill at keeping tabs on their targets too often for him to ignore.

The problem he had was that the memory-stick of records, stolen from the office by his defecting clerk, had been lost. When they caught up with him in Boston and killed him. The killers had been adamant that the stick had not been found on him or in his baggage.

It was pure luck that one of the girls watching him prior to his death had mentioned his brush past the English couple on the quay where they were boarding the *USS Constitution.*

The two events had not been connected at first. By that time the two British people had been off and away.

Regret was not pleased that the muscle he had at his disposal was directed by Russian mafia. Admittedly, Karmelian certainly seemed capable enough. Regret had used him before but he was still trying to understand why the man had not eliminated Abby and Donny when he had had the chance on at least two occasions.

There were too many things being done out of his direct control. He was not accustomed to operating in this way. The problem was that the boss himself had started the arrangements in the 70's, when the importance of laundering the income from illegal sources became necessary for the first time. Up to that time the rules had not been nearly so stringent, nor were they enforced to the same extent as they now were.

Regret picked up his phone. He called the number from memory. When it was answered he said sharply, "Put Karmelian on!"

"Karmelian here." Who is this?"

"Regret! What the devil is going on? I give you a simple job to do and you waste my time while you chase half-way across the country to do something you should have done on day one."

"These kids are no pushover, whatever you think. When my man took them to the gun shop he had no chance to eliminate them. They moment they had guns in their hands they demonstrated they are better than any he had seen with weapons. Since then they have wounded or killed all the men I've sent against them. The contractors all caved in after the guns came out. I am currently planning a proper operation to round them up and when that has been done I will inform you."

"Just make sure this time. I don't do failure, and you had better write that down, because you may be good, but there are others."

"Threatening me could be fatal, Mr Regret. Just remember it takes a lot of money to stop a bullet." The phone went down at that point with enough force to hurt his ear.

Charles Regret shivered. There was menace in the voice that was a warning and a threat. He considered the possibility of having the Russian removed, but decided that the time for that would be when the task he had been set was completed. The phone rang and he considered it for a few moments before picking it up.

"Regret," he said.

At the other end an excited voice said, "I have Mr Barclay on the line."

"Put him through immediately." Regret snapped.

The cultured voice, so familiar, spoke, "Charles, dear boy. Sorry to bother you like this but I seem to be requiring some extra cash for a personal bill. Can you oblige?"

"Of course, sir. How much shall I transfer?"

"Just five mil will be enough. Straight to the current account, I think." The click of the phone breaking the connection signalled the end of the call.

Regret replaced his own handset and sat back in his chair. He rested his elbows on the arms of his chair and tented his fingers in front of him. He reflected. It was time Mr Barclay retired. There were far too many small withdrawals of this type going on. The company could only afford so much. He nodded to himself. *Yes, time to retire Mr Barclay.*

Leaning forward he plucked the phone from its place and stabbed a speed dialled number.

"Yes, Charlie." The voice at the other end of the line was husky from too much drink, cigarettes, whatever?

"Retirement plan, Jennock. Perhaps a burglary gone wrong, I think. Whatever you find in the place you can have." He gave a name and address. "Tonight, I think. Will you manage that?"

"Probably, if the party is present!"

"Good. I'll arrange it." He put the phone down.

At the other end of the line Michael Jennock looked at the address he had written down. He considered. *Good part of town, millionaires even. Probably rent-a-cop security.*

I'll take the Roller, he thought. The black Silver Cloud was a guarantee of entry to most places.

What Addison Barclay thought about the arrival of the Rolls Royce outside his house is not recorded, as he and his guest, later identified as a high-class hooker were in no condition to talk. In fact by the time the bodies were discovered there was no real evidence, except for the obvious scenario carefully staged by Jennock, of the lover's tiff that had gone wrong.

Prior to the decease of said Addison Barclay, he had been persuaded to divulge the combination and the location of the carefully concealed safe. There was enough money therein to make the entire exercise well worth the effort. Jennock's assistant was rewarded with a free extra-curricular service by the hooker, on the mistaken understanding that she would be spared the fate of her client. Sadly she subsequently died during the supposed tiff with her millionaire lover/client?

On receipt of the information that the task had been carried out, Charles Regret transferred the six million dollars already nominated to his own offshore account, to keep the accounting tidy.

***

For Donny and Abby the download from the memory stick was an education. It explained in explicit terms how finance from several major corporations was streamed into alternative accounts and from there into other trades without revealing their true origins. The resulting, apparently legitimate, monies remitted to other banks, less charges and interest, to be used in genuine trading. The person who created the presentation was careful to show the connections of all the major corporations mentioned to criminal organisations.

Donny removed the stick from the USB slot on the laptop. He turned to Abby who was looking thoughtful.

"Well, what do you think?" he asked.

After more thought, Abby turned to him and said, "I can't help thinking that we are in the wrong business!" She laughed. "No wonder they are after us, if they know we have this."

"My guess is that they don't know we have it. They just think we have." Donny smiled. "You do realise that if your handbag was not stuffed with everything bar the kitchen sink we would have found this sooner?"

The assault that followed this remark created an interlude that inevitably ended in a passionate episode that left both temporarily breathless, the subject of the assault forgotten for the moment.

Eventually, Donny returned to the memory stick. "Jonathon?" He suggested.

"I think so." Abby agreed.

While Abby downloaded the files from the stick onto her laptop, Donny got the Sat phone out of its case and called Jonathon at home.

He explained about the memory stick. "Abby is downloading it and she will email it to you direct. Any suggestions regarding the stick itself?"

"Keep it somewhere convenient to ditch. If you are caught with it you will be signing your death warrant. They would never believe that you hadn't taken a look at what's on it. You will need to watch your back. I think the girl and the fake FBI man were opportunist attempts to confirm that the stick had been planted on you. I also think that they are probably two different competing sources. It seems quite clear they will try to eliminate you. I seriously suggest you get on the first plane home. I will be talking to your father and I have no doubt he will agree with me. Leave it now. America will still be there in a year's time. After this has blown over."

"Sorry, Jonathon. I'm having problems with the batteries here. I can't hear you very well. Bye from us both."

"What was that all about?" Abby asked.

"He wants us to go home." Donny said with a shrug. "He thinks they will try to kill us now."

"What does he think they have been doing so far, playing games?" Abby said indignantly.

"You know Jonathon."

"Only too well, and I am suspicious of the interest he is taking about our trip. I don't mean now. I mean ever since we set out. If you recall we were introduced to an FBI agent, albeit a bogus one almost before we started this trip. In addition, remember who set the whole thing up, for our benefit, of course." Abby stopped and thought for a few minutes.

"I am not suggesting that he set us up, but I do think he is taking advantage of the situation. And as far as I'm concerned," she paused and a wicked grin crossed her face, "It does spice up the trip, doesn't it?" Her eyebrows followed her voice as it climbed an octave just a little anxiously.

"Stops it from getting boring, I must say." Donny grinned. "The trouble is, it becomes a habit, all this cloak and dagger stuff. It's going to be difficult getting down to studying again."

"So Durango and the Grand Canyon followed by Las Vegas. Is that the plan?"

"If it's OK with you?"

Abby ran across the room and hugged Donny, who seemed delighted by the attention.

Picking her up in his arms he swung her round laughing as they collapsed on the bed still locked in each other's arms.

When they left the following day there was no sign of the serious inspection that they had given to the surrounding area. As they had drifted around sightseeing, both had paid particular attention to the people around them. They had not anticipated the need when they came to America and up until now, the incidents that had occurred had been almost surreal and apart from normal behaviour, but now having reviewed the events of the past days in the country, the message had been driven home. They had visited the gun shop when they were in Oakley Kansas, following the helicopter incident. There Donny had found a Winchester rifle and ammunition, and a pump action shotgun with an eight round magazine plus a reload magazine. 'Just to even up the odds', as Donny put it.

Abby suggested it went onto the bill for services that she would present to Jonathon. "It was the helicopter," Abby said. "That body falling from the sky drove the message home as far as I was concerned."

"By that time I was convinced as well." Donny agreed, "But I'm still puzzled by the planting of the memory stick. Why should they choose us, whoever they are?"

"The more I think about it the more I believe the whole thing was an off-the-cuff solution to someone's problem. Think about it. You have gone to the trouble to record these details. Why?" She answered her own question. "Blackmail? Or evidence. So suppose you think you are being followed by very nasty people who may think, but don't actually know, that you are stealing their records. You can run but in the end they will catch you. If they find the stick on you then it's a concrete boot and a swim in the river. So you pick somebody you can recognize in the future and slip the stick into a pocket or handbag. You're in the clear if you are caught, and you can identify the current carriers of the stick to recover it."

They were sitting at a table in the Hard Rock Cafe in the centre of town. Both sat quietly thinking about Abby's theory.

"You think the attacks have been from the man trying to recover his property?"

"I think we have been attacked by him, at least people paid by him, but I think we have also been targeted by the group chasing him. Possibly under the mistaken impression that we are working, actually employed by him."

To the onlooker they were two young people without a care in the world. The weapons they both carried were not obvious, but they were there ready for action none the less.

Satisfied, that for the moment they were under the radar, they departed Denver early next morning.

***

The road through the mountains was spectacular and the journey of over two hundred miles was without incident. The town of Durango was interesting to them both, though truth to be told, Donny's interest in the town had developed from the cowboy books he had avidly read when he was younger.

The real relic of that period was the Silverton Railway, complete with antique locomotive and restored carriages. It was also the place where their followers caught up.

It was Donny that spotted him. Both youngsters had acquired cowboy hats, which reduced their profile in a community where everyone wore them. It was also the reason for Donny spotting their tail so quickly.

The man in question was not tall but he was heavily built. Dressed in T-shirt and jeans, he should not have stood out in a community where jeans were everyday wear for the bulk of the population. But this man was tattooed. One entire arm in fact, with coils and shapes of exotic plants.

It was not that there were no tattooed men in Durango. They had sent their share of young men to the services. And many had come back with the odd tattoo. But the extent and subject of the decoration, plus the accent of the man when he spoke, made him stand out in that small community.

"He looks tough," Abby observed.

"It's his friend that concerns me more." Donny observed.

"Friend, you said nothing about a friend. Where is he what does he look like?"

"I don't know, and that's what concerns me," Donny said thoughtfully. "You see, I don't think our trackers are stupid enough to release such an obvious shadow without backup, someone for us to be concerned with, a distraction, while a backup sneaks around behind us to take us by surprise. It would not be the first time something like that happened and I'm sure it won't be the last. So, until I know who he or she is, I'm keeping my options open."

The ride was fun and Donny, who had been an avid Western fan when he was younger, swore he recognized several of the locations along the railway tracks from movies he had actually seen. "It's like Monument valley west of here. They are always filming backgrounds there because the scenery is so spectacular.

Chapter six

They had checked into a hotel on the main street of town and it was there that they spotted their tail's back-up. It was also there that they were joined by Jonathon.

Leaving their hotel to eat that evening at the diner along the street, they realized that there was someone behind them.

Abby said in a normal voice. "Jonathon, you must change your aftershave. It's far too distinctive for the work you are doing."

"Abby, not all people have the acute sense of smell that you enjoy. Besides which, with you two on the loose, I don't need to go out into the field nearly so often. Between you, you cover most of the ground I would normally be occupying."

He caught up with them, walking alongside them and sweeping them past the diner they were aiming for and through the entrance of the Last Chance saloon which, contrary to its colourful name, was actually one of the best restaurants in town.

They were greeted and seated by an attentive waiter who having taken an order for drinks left them alone with a jug of iced water.

"Are you enjoying your vacation in USA?" Jonathon asked.

"We would have been happier if we had not felt that we were being manipulated from the start," Donny retorted. "My feeling is that we were sent here to be targeted as a diversion for some other project. This leads me to believe that you know more about all this than you have been telling us. I am hoping, for the sake of our health, that you are about to give us some form of briefing, at least." He turned to Abby, "Time to put up or shut up I think."

"So, Jonathon. Do we get to know what this is all about? Or do we hop the next plane home?"

The pair directed their attention at the man seated opposite them, who was showing no signs of discomfort or in fact dismay. From the smile on his face it was evident that he was enjoying the meeting, so far at least.

The waiter returned and delivered their drinks and departed once more with their orders.

Having used the diversion to sort things out in his mind, Jonathon started to explain. "In the normal scheme of things you were not intended to get involved at all. Up to the point where our man was identified and intercepted, he got away from his tail and was able to contact me. He was in Boston and I remembered that you were there too. I had no time to brief you, but I sent Peters, our agent, your pictures and suggested he contact you to run interference. Unfortunately he was unable to contact you in time. He followed you from Harvard to the ship, but because he was under observation at the time he was only able to slip the memory stick into Abby's bag. He could not even warn you without setting them on to you. He hoped to be able to ring you and tell you what was happening but he was taken out before he had the chance. They got his phone and were able to get your details from it. You were seen in the area you see. Finding your pictures and de-tails on the phone they put two and two to-gether."

The food arrived and all conversation slowed right down while the trio ate.

"What is this all about?" Abby asked as the tempo of eating slowed down.

Jonathon picked up the last french-fry from his plate and ate it before sitting back with a sigh. "That's the first full meal I've had since I left UK. Now you were asking what this was all about. It is about money-laundering." He lifted his hand to stop the immediate response from them both.

"Before you say a word, I am not talking about odds and ends. I am talking billions of dollars, from here, from Europe, from the Far-East. This is a global business and it is operated on that basis. The economies of some countries are based on laundered monies from drugs, prostitution, protection and all forms of criminal violence. Industrial espionage is a particular corner of the market. But our biggest problem is the banking industry itself. There is evidence that respected high street banks have become involved in this business. You may have noticed that the unsettled state of the banking industry has caused enormous problems with the disclosures of illegal dealing and improper charging, including extortionate fees for service. You may have also noticed that those banks which have been supported with Government and public money, despite supposed huge losses, are still also achieving huge profits, sometimes only in certain aspects of their business.

"The fact is that ill-advised politicians have been suggesting separating these profitable sections from the mainline business of the bank, rather than applying these profits to the debts the banks have incurred. This merely highlights their naiveté, and or cupidity, depending on the source of their publicised opinions.

"That is the background. The memory stick contained records of a series of transactions that, if exposed to the public, would create panic in the financial world and havoc with the public.

"Your preservation of that memory stick has been a vital part of our operation in this field. The detail on that memory has been secured now, but the people after you do not know that. They know their security has been breached, but they are not aware that our only contact with that breach has been eliminated. They are under the impression that you also are part of the group that created the breach. So you are very much a current target for the organisation we are trying to get rid of."

"We are trying to get rid of? Who is we? Are we talking about the usual suspects, FBI, Treasury, CIA, in addition to M16 and the Surete?" The sardonic tone in Donny's voice left no doubt of his feelings in the matter of the combined efforts of the alphabet soup that Jonathon himself was a part of.

"I know what you think. But we are talking truly international now, and they all must be involved as well as a few you haven't mentioned. So that is what is happening and we would prefer you to stay ahead of the opposition for the rest of your time in USA but not too far ahead. We would prefer you keep them occupied while we continue to dig in their back garden, as it were. We are in fact keeping a fatherly eye on you both so there is less risk of them causing you harm."

"He's pulling our leg, isn't he?" Abby said to Donny. "It must be a joke! Keeping an eye on us? What about our followers here in Durango, then? Are they your people or the oppositions? If they are yours, then I would rather they were sent somewhere else. If they are opposition, I'm happy because they are even more inept that the Russians on the east coast."

"Russians? Are you saying there are still Russians following you? Here?"

Donny looked at Jonathon pityingly. "In the corner of the room beside the pot palm, talking to the woman."

Jonathon turned casually. He shook his head. "You are surely not talking about that dark-haired dish in the corner sitting with the big, blond fellow in the Armani suit.

"The blond bit comes off actually. That is the man we called Yul Brunner in disguise."

"Things have moved faster that I realised. My apologies, kids. I will arrange you return home as soon as we can get a flight out."

Abby laughed. "Jonathon you are priceless. You know damn well that there is no way that Donny and I would duck out now. Here we are in the middle of things. What could turn out to be a much less boring holiday than we imagined and you want to spoil it for us. In your dreams, Jonathon, in your dreams. Now, you have done your duty. You have tried to dissuade us and failed. Now is the time for the fall-back plan. Brief us carefully, and properly with all the information you have."

Jonathon looked at them helplessly, then threw up his hands. "You father will kill me if he finds out."

"So don't tell him."

"But he is bound to ask how you are doing."

"Tell him. Your son is enjoying his sojourn in North America and looking quite fit and well. Abby is having a ball at the museums and we looking forward to visiting Monument Valley and the Grand Canyon. There, that should do it. Didn't take long, did it?"

Jonathon looked at them both doubtfully. "Are you both sure you want to go through with this. Really sure?"

Abby laughed. "Wonderful, Jonathon. Are you considering going to Hollywood? I'm sure you could make a great living as an actor. Look at me, and convince me that you did not have this planned as soon as things went wrong for your agent in place here!"

Jonathon looked seriously back at the smiling face in front of him. He shrugged giving in finally. "Well, I did hope things would work out that way. But I did mean what I said about going home if you would rather."

Donny said "Now that is settled, let's just enjoy what's left of this food and plan our next move. I was thinking we would go to Grand Canyon via Monument Valley. I would like to do some photography in both places if we can make the time."

They returned to their hotel after eating and spent the next hour planning how they could take in the sights, and at the same time ward off any attempt to kidnap or otherwise interfere with their liberty.

The fact that 'Yul Brunner and girlfriend' were here already and that it was unlikely to be a coincidence meant that they were probably being set up for an ambush.

The car they were currently driving still had the guns they had acquired, locked in the trunk.

Yul Brunner or to give him his real name Karmelian was angry. This whole business was taking too long. The stupid bitch he had been saddled with had insisted on being entertained in the best hotel in Durango, and he was damned sure the targets had spotted them, though they had not given any sign that they had noticed them.

The other thing that was bothering him was the tattooed man who was following them. He suspected that Regret was having them followed to make sure the job was done and then to clean up afterwards. If he was right in this assumption Mr Regret was going to live up to his name. Karmelian had not gained his reputation by being stupid. Survival in this business was a basic requirement, and in the event of any conflict it was the quick that survived and intelligence was worth more than bullets. The photograph of the tattooed man had already brought results. Michael Jennock was known in the business. Like Karmelian he was known for getting things done. Currently Karmelian was thinking about having a discussion with Jennock on the subject of the arrogant Mr Regret. It could be possible that Jennock may also be offended by Mr Regret's demands and manners. He shrugged after all they were both professionals.

The voice through the communicating door said, "Are you going out?"

He replied evenly, "I was not anticipating it. Why?" His spoken voice had long been trained to the cultured restrained tones of the east coast, upper classes.

"I wondered if we might discuss matters without the continual hassle that has kept us on the move over the past three days."

The pair had spent most of the time travelling, and however attractive the two people may be, neither had made any suggestion of interest in the other. So it was a surprise for Karmelian to find that Karla was in fact in her nightgown sitting on the bed when he entered her room.

He was in shirtsleeves and slacks after showering, comfortable in his bare feet. When he saw her he shrugged and said, "My apologies. I was getting ready for bed."

Shirley smiled "As you may have noticed so was I." She held out her hand to him. "Come and join me over here. It is more comfortable than the chair."

As he seated himself on the bed beside her he said, "Aw hell, why not!" And buried his face in her inviting bosom as she sank back with her arms about him.

The phone rang two hours later, waking the pair. Karla picked it up. "Mr Regret for you, madam." The voice of the receptionist was followed by the urbane tones of Regrets voice. "Well, what is happening? Has there been any progress since you last reported?"

"There have been one or two things. As you know we are now in Grand Canyon and we are anticipating action tomorrow." Seeing that Karmelian was awake she thought possibly there might be some more action tonight, but she kept that to herself. Noticing the time was after midnight she added, "What made you call at this time of night. I have been travelling for the past two days and you couldn't be bothered to allow me to sleep through to morning?" She was getting annoyed, and to her surprise Regret apologized. He had not considered the time difference between the east coast and Arizona.

Karla turned to her partner. "What about that? He apologized for waking me up, now I will have trouble getting back to sleep. How about you?" She slipped down into his open arms and kissed him just because she wanted to. He responded dutifully as any gentleman would.

When they had left Durango, Jonathon phoned Abby's cell to let them know that Yul Brunner and his friend Karla were on their tail. Also a pick-up had left after their Russian friends, with the tattooed man and a companion; he could not make out if the companion was a man or a woman. "Be careful!" were his last words before he rang off.

Donny, with his camera out, caught glimpses of their two sets of followers as he wandered about getting pictures of some of the more spectacular buttes located through the enormous stretch of the valley. He made no effort to conceal what he was doing, and Abby who was sitting in the shade of the car nursing the treasured Winchester waited in vain for some attempt at interference from either of the following vehicles.

In fact both passed without stopping and disappeared in the direction of the Grand Canyon. She concluded that they had both decided that an ambush further down the road was a more practical proposition.

The journey to Grand Canyon Village where they were booked into the Lodge, took the rest of the day. They arrived late mainly due to the efforts by Donny to cover the grandeur of the country with a selection of photographs.

Despite the late hour of their arrival Donny was up early to see the sunrise over the Canyon and by 9.00 a.m., he had booked them both on a mule trip down into the canyon below for the following day.

There was enough to occupy the two young people in the village itself and the time passed swiftly. They spotted both sets of followers during their leisurely sightseeing, though they gave nothing away and the followers showed no obvious interest.

Karmelian staged his meeting with Jennock when both were alone in the men's room of the Grand Canyon Museum.

As they stood addressing the porcelain Karmelian said, "Regret send you?"

Jennock looked at his companion and decided it was pointless playing games. "Yes, he did, and you?" He knew the answer of course but it was something to say.

"Let's talk in the café."

They both washed, left the room and found a corner table where they could talk quietly without being overheard.

"They are going into the Canyon tomorrow morning. I thought I might take them out then."

"Sounds good to me." Jennock said

"Worked for Regret before?" Karmelian asked.

"A few times." Jennock replied.

"Terminations, I guess?" Karmelian suggested. "Which brings me to the point of this conversation. I think you have been tasked with tidying up after my companion and I have done our job?"

"Maybe!" Jennock gave nothing away.

"Who is your friend?" Karmelian said casually.

"Some trainee that Regret pushed on to me. Getting experience, he said."

"Your trainee has just spent seven years in Delta force. He knows as much about sudden death as the pair of us. My partner knows him from her own service in Afghanistan. She was a Seal."

Jennock winced. "You thinking what I'm thinking?"

Karmelian nodded "I guess. I think my lady has decided to join me in my retirement plan. How about you? A call on Mr Regret perhaps, after the job?"

Jennock contemplated the suggestion. Then "I think that would be a good idea. I'll report completion of mission with the regretful story of the death of my companion. How does that sound?"

"Makes sense to me!" Karmelian agreed and he shook the extended hand of his fellow assassin.

Neither man trusted the other to keep his word. But both realized that whatever happened afterwards, the job had to come first. It was a matter of pride.

Chapter seven

They left the rim at 7.30am. The mules were small but they were fresh and sure-footed. The trail downward was not steep to begin with but it took time for the riders to get accustomed to the giddy depths that were periodically appearing dramatically, seemingly directly underneath the small hooves of their mounts.

A helicopter passed them after they had been riding for an hour. The guide, Maximilian Gomez, had called a halt for a coffee break and a chance to photograph some of the dramatic scenery. Donny, having become accustomed to the mule's gait, had been filming, using his small video camera, capturing the feeling of the perilous journey as they zigzagged down the historic trail. Working on the basis that the mule knew the way better than he did, having achieved some harmony with the movement of the beast, he spent most of the time now just rocking to the rhythm of the mules pace, using both hands to operate his cameras in turn.

At the point where they had stopped, Max said, "From here on, one hand for the camera one for the reins. Entendido, Senor? You understand?"

Donny looked as if he might protest, but a look and a slight shake of her head from Abby convinced him not to argue. After all it was possible that the opposition might be planning to take them out here in the canyon, so it really made sense.

"Max, the helicopter that passed us. Where would he be going? There does not seem any space to land hereabouts."

"Another hour down the trail there is a parking area cleared on an outcrop. It is a camp site if we get caught by bad weather, and a place where the helicopters land for their passengers to take photographs and experience the heat here in the canyon. Hold it!"

Donny was moving to take a picture of the group of mules and people standing and sitting together on the wide section of the trail when Max gave his warning. He stopped and froze, his eye darting round to see what was wrong.

Max drew the carbine he had in his saddle holster. He cocked it and aimed past the rigid figure of Donny. Donny slowly turned his head. A cougar was standing on the trail eying the group of mules and people, tail swishing from side to side. Max fired and the cougar vanished unhurt. The mules had begun to show signs of distress, but settled down with the disappearance of the threat and the tour continued down the trail.

Abby, riding beside Donny on one of the wider sections commented, "Did you notice that the mules didn't turn a hair at the shot when Max fired at the cougar?"

Donny looked across at her with a smile. "And what made you think I had any interest in the mules at that time. I did have a cougar eying me like a breakfast prospect?"

Abby continued, "Max was saying that there are occasions like today when having the carbine makes the difference between life and death, and the reason why the mules are accustomed to the sound of the carbine."

The bullet sang past Donny's ear. The report followed, echoing around the canyon back and forth. The second bullet was almost lost in the echoes of the first, its report combining with the fading echo of the first shot. Neither had any effect because Donny was down, hidden by the width of the trail along with all the others on the trip.

Max said, "Damn hunters. They shoot at the animal without thinking where they are pointing the gun." He raised his carbine and fired twice over the rim of the trail. "Maybe that will suggest that they are endangering people. He stood up and walked to the edge of the trail, looked down and swore. "Guys in an all-terrain vehicle down on the lower ridge. They think it's fun to scare the tourists. Can't see their tails for dust now.

Okay, folks. Come on up, the danger is over; let's mount-up and get down the hill, times-a-wastin'."

At the foot of the trail the group stood on the floor of the canyon, gazing around them in amazement. On the way down things had been spectacular, now there were no words left to describe it. The mighty river had carved another groove from the rock and the trail continued down to the river's edge. At the insistence of the group Max led them the rest of the way down where the cooler air in the shadow where the sun had not yet reached rose up to greet them. On the river bank they rested and set up the camp for the night.

Charles Regret was angry. He was not accustomed to being kept waiting too long when he arranged matters with the professional help. After all, that's what they were, professional. It was their job. Now he had two teams in the field and nothing was happening.

He dialed Karmelian's cell phone the screen lit up, 'Off Line'. He tried Jennock, with the same result. *Where the hell are they both?* he thought, slamming the telephone down. He had the feeling that this was not going well. He decided that maybe he had better go and be there; just to be sure they shot the right people. Then he would shoot them.

Among the other touristsm Donny and Abby felt on the one hand protected and on the other guilty for placing them in danger of collateral damage.

It was for this reason that they decided that the sooner they distanced themselves from the others in the party the better for everyone. They ate their food quickly in the gloom of the canyon and then drifted off down alongside the rushing waters of the Colorado River.

There were disadvantages for them in this because they could hear nothing except the river. No chance of hearing footsteps or even shots at this level, the rocky riverbed at this point made sure of that. However as they wandered down the path along the riverbank they came to a spot where the canyon widened and there was a stretch of open ground with scrubby bushes growing. The river was wider here and the current was slower with the funnelling effect reduced.

They sat down and studied the surrounding area searching for vantage points that overlooked the spot. Abby said, "I think we are alone here, completely alone!" She shivered. Donny put his arms round her drawing her close.

"I have a suggestion to make." He said with a small smile. His fingers undid the top button of her blouse, "How about…" His fingers undid the second button. "How about we cuddle close and keep warm." He bent his head and kissed the swell of her breast.

She put her hand on the back of his head and held him close whispering, "Two men have come into sight. They are carrying rifles. When they get near enough I will let you go. We can take them out together." She chuckled for effect saying, for the benefit of the watchers, "That tickles. You should have brought a shaver."

Donny growled and burrowed deeper. "I think I will just eat you instead."

Abby said, "Now would be a good time." Donny rolled over drawing the Walther aiming but not firing at the two men who were staring at Abby's mostly exposed breasts.

They were not the people who had been following them. Their rifles were hunting rifles and both had telescopic sights. They were young, maybe mid-twenties in plaid shirts and jeans, with flat heeled boots and cowboy hats.

Abby closed her blouse with the hand that was not holding her gun.

"Did you two have some business here?" She said coolly.

"N-no. We were just cruising looking for game, but, wow, ma'am, we did not wish to disturb you."

The second man smiled and said to Donny, "You can put that toy gun away, son. If we decide to look after your friend here, that ain't going to stop anything at this range. Lady, why don't you open up again? That was a mighty fine sight for a poor country boy like me."

His friend looked at him with horror. "What the hell?"

His companion said, "Hey, don't you see these are the two people those guys were looking for, the fugitives from justice. We've landed lucky here. Apart from the reward we can have a little fun here. He swung his rifle round to bring it to bear on the couple still on the ground. "I'm feeling pretty horny after seeing this little girl here. I'll be seeing about that right now. You can have the boy if you'd rather."

Abby looked bored and stood up and stretched. Both men gawked at the sight of her toned figure. Donny shot the mouthy man who looked stunned and dropped his rifle as his arm suddenly broke. "What th.... damn!" He said and clutched the wound with his other hand.

His friend looked shocked and lowered his rifle. "I don't understand," he said, "Charlie has never done anything like this before."

"Put the rifle down." Abby said quietly. As he complied, she walked over to Charlie who was sitting looking at his broken arm with a dazed look on his face. She untied the bandanna from around his neck and studied his wound. "Keep holding it like that." To the other man she said, "Find me some straight sticks."

Donny came over with the other rifle while the uninjured man scrabbled among the bushes looking for sticks. Abby tore the bandanna in half. When the sticks were produced she selected the straightest, then wrapped the torn bandanna around the wounds. With quick fingers she undid the belt round the wounded man's waist and used it to tie the sticks round the broken arm.

Charlie said, "Thanks!" Then he spoke again. "They said you were both wanted for murder and armed robbery, and if we caught you we could have you before we took you in. But if we killed you that would be alright, too. He had a badge, FBI, otherwise....." His voice tailed off.

His friend said "There were four of them, three men and a woman; suits you know, button-down shirts, black Oxford shoes. They said since we were flying down here to keep an eye open for you."

"How are you getting back?" Donny asked.

"The copter is calling for us here." He waved around him at the wide area beside the river. "The pilot said that there was room here and providing there was no storm or mist he could manage with his landing lights. That sounds like him now." The murmur of an engine became louder as it reflected from the walls of the canyon, and the whup, whup of the rotating blades approached the clearing. The light suddenly blazed and illuminated the two hunters; of Donny and Abby there was no sign. The aircraft came to rest settling gently to the ground and the rotors stopped spinning. The ticking of the cooling engine was clear over the sound of the river.

Two men descended from the helicopter and walked over to the hunters still on the ground.

"What happened? Did you find them?"

Donny and Abby rose from their cover behind the helicopter, silently checking to see if there was anyone inside. There was a man tied up under the control of a woman who held a gun.

Abby whispered, "Its Karla, Yul Brunner's girl. I'll take her, you get the man out." She carefully opened the door behind Karla and her hand shot forward grabbing the gun in her hand, twisting it out of her grip and backhanding the woman at the same time. "Sit still and shut up, Karla, or whatever your name is." She reinforced her request with the pressure of the pistol to Karla's neck.

Donny who had now climbed into the cabin was untying the man on the back seat.

As the man opened his mouth to speak, Donny said, "Shut up, or I'll put the gag back in."

Getting the message the man closed his mouth and waited while Donny completed releasing him. "Now into the pilot's seat and sit tight."

The man cautiously got out and slid into the front seat of the helicopter.

Beside the bank of the river, the two men were interrogating the hunters. One of the newcomers bent down and nudged Charlie's broken arm.

Charlie screamed and Donny stepped forward. "Are you looking for me?" He said it just loud enough. The young man, bent over Charlie, spun round lifting a Glock automatic. He was flung into the water by the impact of the bullet, and swept away along the canyon out of sight into the narrowing channel, his weakly waving arm the last sight they had of him.

Karmelian silently shrugged his shoulders—Jennock's young man who had undoubtedly been sent to tidy up. He had been just too quick for his own health it seemed. He was content to wait for Jennock to appear; once that happened he would take his chances.

"What are you after, Mister whoever-you-are?" Donny asked.

In the helicopter the situation had changed slightly. Karla Peters was now tied up and lying on the floor of the machine, with a tape over her mouth. The pilot was crouched down out of the line of sight. Abby was outside, following Jennock who was creeping up toward Donny and the man they had called Yul Brunner. She was careful to keep quiet and made sure of Jennock, who had left the helicopter to make a complete sweep of the area before joining his partner, he should have finished with the hunters by now. He had not been aware that Donny and Abby were here though he had heard the shot and realized as he approached Karmelian that something was wrong. He had his gun pointed at whoever was standing with his colleague.

"Where has Steve gone?" He called.

Karmelian was baffled for a moment then realized Jennock was referring to his young partner. "He went for a swim!"

Puzzled, Jennock said, "Who is the guy with you?" He had not seen the gun Donny was holding.

"Actually!" Said Abby behind him, "He is my boyfriend, and this is a gun lined up on your back. It's just like the one he has lined up on your friend."

Jennock shrugged and lowered his own gun. "Just toss it down where you are and go and join the party," Abby said coolly. "Please don't think I might miss at this range, or even that I might hesitate."

Something about the tone made Jennock change his mind about trying to jump his captors.

He walked over and joined Karmelian.

Donny said, "I was wondering where you had got to. What happened to the woman?"

"I'll fetch her." Abby ran back to the helicopter and tugged out the pilot who then dragged out the woman, Karla, and released her feet. All three then walked over to the river bank and joined the others.

Steve, who had been swept off downriver was not feeling his best. The bullet had missed his lung, but, only just, he guessed. It hurt like hell even with the deadening effect of the cold water. He knew he had to get out of the water as quickly as possible otherwise hypothermia would kill him as effectively as a bullet. Nearly three miles passed before he managed to drag himself out on to the river bank. He started walking upriver immediately. There was no other way to fight off the cold and, despite the crippling pain from his wound, his training would not allow him to give up without a battle.

By the time he made it to the landing place there was no one there. The helicopter had long gone, so he kept walking. He reached Max's camp when he was on the verge of final collapse.

Donny and Abby, having relieved their prisoners of the other weapons carried undeclared by the trio, tied them all with items of their clothing torn into strips.

Abby wrote a note to Max and wrapped it round a rock, and they all boarded the helicopter for the trip back to village.

They dropped the rock down to Max who opened the note while they hovered. He waved to them and they flew out of the canyon.

At the airfield, when they landed, all six of them went into the company office. The pilot got a bottle of bourbon out of the drawer of his desk and started pouring drinks. As Donny reached for the phone Karmelian spoke, "Before you do anything like reporting us, there are things you need to know."

Donny turned and looked at him, "So, what do I need to know?"

"I need some assurance that you will let us go before I say anything. But if you value your lives you will want to hear what I have to say."

Jennock and Karla looked at Karmelian curiously. They had no idea what he was planning but they would wait and see what he was up to.

Donny nodded. "Right. If what you have to say is worth it I will let you loose, with the proviso that I will shoot you on sight if I find you attempting to follow or interfere with us in any way.

"That's reasonable," Karmelian said. "With that in mind, I guess you realize that our being here was nothing personal. We are here because we were paid to be here. We had also worked out between us that we were scheduled to be hit the moment we had carried out our task."

"Killing Abby and me?" Donny asked.

Karmelian nodded. "That was what I was hired to do back in Detroit, though I was supposed to find you, and interrogate you before that. From Chicago onward you were scheduled for a hit.

"The guy who set it up is named Regret, Charles Regret, a banker in a private bank that launders money for the various variety of mobs that we suffer in this land of opportunity." He smiled. "As you are personally aware, I failed up to now, though I did expect to win in the end. The reason we have been chasing you both has something to do with the bank. I was told to search you both, and find a memory stick that Regret thinks you have. If I found it I was expected to return it to Regret, for an extra bonus.

"Now my colleagues and I have worked out that we are scheduled to be eliminated, we decided that we would collect our fee and then pay Mr Regret a visit. Seeing things have changed," he shrugged and a wry smile crossed his face, "We decided that a change of employer might be a good idea. We would still contemplate a visit to see Mr Regret, before we retired finally if that were possible."

Neither Jennock nor Karla made any comment.

"Where would we find this Charles Regret?" Abby asked.

"New York, though I have a feeling that he might not be there at the moment. He sounded pretty pissed when we spoke last."

Donny wrote down the address and the name of the Bank, and passed the note to Abby.

She picked up the phone looking at the pilot with an eyebrow raised. He shrugged and said "Help yourself."

She rang Jonathon on the number he had given them, and passed the information on to him.

Within ten minutes the phone rang. Abby picked up. It was Jonathon. "He has gone from home. The treasury boys are in the bank at the moment doing their thing, but Mr. Regret has gone. It looks as if he may be within shooting distance since we have found a booking for Las Vegas in his wastebasket. If he used it, he has been there for two days already. Take care, you two. He could be seriously nasty considering what he thinks you have done to his comfortable life."

There was nothing Donny and Abby could do with their three prisoners so, after ensuring that they boarded a flight east, they departed south then west to Lake Mead and Las Vegas.

Chapter Eight

Both Donny and Abby had seen the pictures. They had, over the past few years, seen the movies and were prepared, they thought, for the impact of the desert city.

They weren't! It was evening when they arrived. The sun had set and the desert night fell like a sparkling curtain everywhere but ahead. There the explosion of multi-coloured lights wiped the sky in a great arc around it. They entered the bubble of light and sound, driving the length of the main street before doing a U-turn and returning.

They checked in at the Jockey Club, handed the car keys to the valet and followed their porter to the elevators. The noise was continuous, but there was a buzz about the place that was exciting to them both.

The room was quiet. The silence had started in the elevator, but when the elevator moved it was silence all the way. Abby commented, "It's eerie. The noise has been switched off like a light."

Their porter laughed, "It gets everyone that way. The boss said that the noise should be tapered off as the elevator rose, but the sound guys just couldn't do it, all or nothing. So the boss decided nothing!"

The room telephone rang. Donny lifted it and a voice said, "Mr Weston, the management of the Jockey Club welcome you to our Inn. You and your lady are invited to a welcoming supper buffet in the dining room on the 1st floor of the Inn anytime in the next hour as our guests. Thank you for choosing The Jockey Club."

"They don't waste time, do they?" Abby commented. "I'm for the shower." She dashed off, dropping clothes on her way to the bathroom.

Donny followed, rescuing the clothing and dumping them in the laundry basket, before undressing himself and joining Abby in the shower.

The dining room was not as crowded as the salon where the machines were busy, apparently all the time. The gambling tables were located at the rear of the room with the conveniently situated dining area, alongside.

They were greeted by an Armani-suited man who spoke to them by name and introduced himself as Michael Clark, Chef de Salon of the hotel. A click of the fingers and a waitress appeared.

She escorted them to a table introducing herself as Eileen and invited them to order drinks, which in the restaurant were all on the house. She waved a hand at the buffet table covered with enough food it seemed to ease the famine in Ethiopia for a week.

Eileen returned with their drinks and leaned down to ensure that Donny receive the full bene-fit of her surgically-enhanced bosom. The mini-mal Basque she was wearing left little to the imagination, barely covering the area between fishnet tights and aforementioned bosom. When she left Abby giggled, looked at her own neatly proportioned figure, and said. "They do like to give value for money here, don't they?"

Donny blushed! It had been a creditable per-formance on the part of Eileen. It also seemed to be part of the exciting atmosphere generated here.

The drinks that arrived had been accompa-nied by a stack of chips each. Ten ten-dollar chips each. Donny nodded thoughtfully. There was no doubt a lot of thought had gone into the selling of this place.

Charles Regret had already been in Las Ve-gas for nearly two days. He had not really been certain that the two troublesome people would be coming here but it was a reasonable assumption.

They were apparently here on holiday. Having driven across the country to the Grand Canyon, where else would they go next?

He had checked into the Paris Hotel, its central location making it useful for the search needed to locate the boy, Weston, and his girlfriend. He had hired a selection of leg-men to carry out the search. The bank had contacts all over the United States, and Las Vegas was particularly well served with villains, both syndicate and free-lance. Initially the men were tasked to locate the couple. They had names and photographs taken during the pathetic debacles involving his erstwhile employees on the trail between the east coast and here.

There was a factor that Regret had not counted on. Neither the fugitives nor Regret realized that the survivors of the Grand Canyon episode were also arriving in Las Vegas, just about an hour after Donny and Abby were checking in.

The small group travelled together, having decided that since they were not about to get paid for their efforts so far and since they had been marked for elimination, if and when they had completed their tasks, they decided that Charles would regret his decision to dispose of them.

So while Regret was chasing Donny and Abby, Karmelian, Karla and Jennock were chasing Regret.

The location of Regret was easy to establish. His arrival at the Paris Hotel was hardly a secret. In the circumstances he was a victim of his own legend. In his position at the bank he had allowed his arrogance to show. Though he was well-known and could command attention, he was not liked.

For a person like Karmelian, finding him was easy. His own reputation had developed through the cultivation of helpful contacts. He was one of those people who paid his bills promptly and tipped generously. Most important of all he thanked people who performed services for him.

At the 'Circus, Circus' Hotel he spoke briefly to the receptionist as they checked in. In their suite he told the others that Regret was in the Paris Hotel and that he had hired muscle to find Donny Weston and Abby Marshall.

"We're lucky; the word is on the street, and it includes the fact that Regret has put it out. That does mean we have time to find and warn the two youngsters."

"I thought we were going to finish that job?" Karla said, eyebrow raised.

"Do you think we would ever get paid for it?" Jennock asked with an amused smile.

"I think we should remember that we are still here because the two youngsters did not kill us when they had the opportunity." Karmelian said seriously.

"That was just weakness!" Karla said defensively.

"Six dead, four wounded and three beaten-up, what part of weakness does that display?" Karmelian was serious. "There is a time to be grateful for small mercies. They could have handed us our heads, and dumped us in the Colorado River. Be grateful they didn't. They could have called in the law. They didn't. Wake up, Karla. Be happy to be still alive. If the chance comes to return the favor, I will. How about you, Jennock?"

"I'm with you. Let's get this show on the road. There should be enough eyes on the street. We know where Regret is. Let's find the youngsters, and warn them."

It was Karla who spotted them. She was cruising south down The Boulevard and she noticed Abby coming out of the Jockey Club, bag in hand heading for the store down street from the hotel.

Karla pulled over and honked the horn. Abby walked over warily. Karla held up her hands in a gesture to show she was not armed. "If you are going shopping, I'll give you a lift. But I really stopped you to warn you that Charles

Regret is in town. He has put out the word for you to be lifted and brought in."

Abby slid into the car. "Why are you telling me this? Why should it worry you that Charles Regret is after us?"

Karla looked at Abby seriously, then started the car and drove off down the Boulevard. "Karmelian pointed out that but for you two we could all be floating down the Colorado River without a boat. Like you, we are all on Regret's 'Shit list'. This means to all intents and purposes we, I mean all of us, are living on borrowed time.

"It is in our mutual interest to lift that threat. We have not been paid for the work we undertook for him, and considering the fact that Regret targeted you two from the beginning, I guess you also have a reason to remove the threat that he poses."

Abby sat thinking. "Where are you based?"

"'Circus Circus'!" Karla's answer was immediate and Abby guessed, honest.

"Right take me back to the Jockey Club and drop me off. Donny and I will make a point of dropping in this evening. We will be tooled up. I'm promising nothing, but we will call this evening," The car drew up outside the Jockey Club and Abby got out.

"Later!" Karla called, as if they were old friends.

Abby waved smiling to Karla as if they had been friends for years, and turned to walk into the hotel.

Karla saw the lift in her rear-view mirror. She keyed her phone. Karmelian picked up. "Yes Karla?"

Abby just got lifted at the Jockey Club. We have spoken and she agreed to come to the hotel tonight. I am following a black Galaxy with tinted windows. She reeled off the number. It looks as if we are heading to the desert, south coming up to the airport."

"We are on our way to back you up. Jennock is at the airport now. I'll call him now and try and get Donny on the way. Good work, Karla. Stay safe."

The pick-up truck driven by Jennock joined the chase from the airport turnoff. Karla noticed it and recognised it. She was relieved because she noticed another car joining the parade that also had tinted windows that closed up behind the Galaxy and maintained station with it, turning off down a dirt road leading to a derelict building, off the road, about two hundred yards on the right.

Both Karla and Jennock kept going, pulling over and turning at the turnoff to Sloan according to the sign. Driving back they turned into the dirt road for the next door lot and parked.

Jennock beeped the GPS coordinates to Karmelian who was en-route to join them.

Abby stayed cool. The two men and the woman, who had lifted her, had not even searched her. She realized that they had not been told the history of the relationship between Donny, herself, and Charles Regret. Considering her position she decided that the time was not yet right to change their opinion. She turned to the man who seemed to be leading the group, and said, "Just what the hell do expect to get for kidnapping me? I have no money nor has my family. What is this all about?"

Shut up, woman. You will soon find out. The door of the other car closed and they heard the footsteps coming to the house door.

The leader nodded to the nearest man who leaned across and opened the door for the visitor.

It revealed Jennock with a gun in his hand. He did not hesitate. He shot both the doorman and the leader. The woman screamed "Nooooo.." and raised her hands.

The third man had pulled his gun and was aiming at Jennock when Abby's gun cracked and the bullet took him in the head. He collapsed against the wall and slid to the floor leaving a trail of blood and matted down the wall.

Jennock stepped through the door fully at a nod from Abby. His eyes swept the room taking in the three downed men and the woman with her hands up. Abby stepped over and frisked the woman, removing the blade from her thigh sheath, but no other weapon.

Karla walked in. She looked at Abby. "All right? I saw them lift you as I drove off and called for help."

"Thanks," said Abby. "They had not even bothered to search me. I was just wondering who I should shoot first when you walked in."

Jennock disarmed both the men he had shot. "Vests he said laconically. Both men had been knocked over by the close range bullets but neither had actually been wounded. He rose to his feet and turned to Karla.

The leader had recovered and his hand moved down to his ankle slowly. Nobody noticed until he actually drew the short-nosed revolver from an ankle holster. He grimaced and Abby noticed him as he raised the gun to aim at Jennock.

Without conscious thought Abby's left hand raised the knife she had taken from the woman prisoner and threw it. It took the man in the neck, severing his carotid artery causing a jet of blood to shoot out across the room. The cocked gun dropped to the floor, and lay there. The dying man seemed to be looking at it, as if he was wondering how it got there. Then he was dead.

Abby felt sick. It was horrible. First the man she had shot, then this man. She was nearly sick on the spot. She swayed, and Karla caught her, steadying her. "Take it easy," Karla said. "Let's get out of here." She steered Abby out of the door into the sunlight.

Jennock joined them, steering the two survivors in front of him. The woman had a bloodstain across the front of her dress. Abby thought idly it looked as though it was part of the pattern. The door of the second car opened and Karmelian stepped out gun in hand, followed by another man who was looking rather angry and not all bothered.

"You guys are all dead, you realize. Nobody ever lifts a gun on Pirello."

"Shut your mouth creep." To Abby's surprise, it was Karla who spoke to the man. "Pimps like you make me sick."

Pirello opened his mouth to speak again and she slapped him round the face with the gun she still held.

He put his hand to his bruised face but said nothing.

Karla turned to the others. "This is not Regret's operation. Pirello is a pimp. Prostitution is his business. He targets girls, especially foreign girls, here to work or on vacation.

"He rents or sells them to the brothels or other street pimps. If he knew about Regret he might well have sold Abby to him, but I guess this snatch was normal business to Pirello."

Karmelian turned to the woman. "What do you do here?"

She shrugged. "The lady is correct, Pirello is the pimp. I am kept to groom the girls once they have been broken in by the men."

"Broken in?" Karmelian asked.

"They rape them several times. Then they inject the difficult ones with heroin, get them hooked. They are either too ashamed or too dependent to go back to their old lives. I try to smooth out the path for them, make it easier for them to survive. The foreign girls are usually more casual about sex than many of the American girls, so it makes it easier to start them off." She shrugged. "It's a living, and it keeps me off the streets."

Abby looked at her with horror. Her earlier disgust at the shooting and blood suddenly seemed to fall into perspective. She still was not happy about it, but it did not seem as bad as it felt at the time.

Donny arrived and came over to her looking anxiously into her eyes. "Okay?" He asked.

"I am now," she said and slid thankfully into his arms.

"What do we do with them, now we have them?" Donny spoke quietly to Karmelian.

Karmelian sighed. "Leave them to me." He held his hand up as Donny started to protest.

"I have no intention of killing them off, though I would point out that is what they would have done to you and me. And you know what they would have done to Abby. I will deal with this." He turned to Jennock. "Round them up. The Galaxy I think, and call your contact at police HQ. Any suggestions for the location would be helpful. You know this City better than I do."

Jennock grinned, "I know just the place."

Donny and Abby left the building with Karla who drove them back to the Jockey Club.

"I'll call for you tonight. We can go visit the Paris Casino to see what our target looks like." She dropped them at the door and drove off with a flourish, flooring the throttle just for the hell of it and attracting the attention of everyone in the vicinity.

Donny and Abby were inside the Club while the dust was still rising. Nobody in the area noticed them.

Back in their room Donny commented. "That Karla is a shrewd cookie. Nobody bothered with our arrival. They were all too busy watching her departure."

"I'm going down to check out the gambling tables. If we are going to a big casino this evening, I want to know what I'm doing without trying to pick it up as we go along. Would you care to join me?"

"I don't think so. I will have to sort out something to wear tonight. I guess Karla will be dressed to kill so I'm going to give her some competition."

Donny pulled her into his arms. "You could go naked and she would not outshine you!"

Abby giggled. "If I went naked you're probably right. But I am too shy to try that out, so I'll just have to settle for a dress."

With Abby in his arms the casino and practice were forgotten. It was a shock when the phone rang some considerable time later, and Karmelian enquired if they were ready for their evening excursion.

So the dress selection came down to the handiest item in the wardrobe and for Donny, black tie and tuxedo thrown on at the last minute.

In the lobby the group met; Karmelian dapper in tux and a dark wig with grey touched in, looking almost conservative. Karla in a scarlet gown cut low enough but still fashionably decorous, looked stunning. Both looked relaxed and pleased to see the two young people apparently unaffected by their experiences earlier.

The car was waiting when they reached the street. Jennock opened the doors for the two couples to get in. "I'll be parked and ready. Ring twice on the cell, I won't pick up, but I'll be at the door in less than one minute. Ring more than three times and I'll attend with company."

Donny looked at Karmelian with a raised eyebrow.

Karmelian said, "Jennock favors the sawn-off shotgun as company. Personally, I have found that I prefer Karla these days." He looked at her and grinned. She smiled back at him wickedly. "What he means is he prefers this." She lifted her long skirt to reveal her long legs with a glimpse of matching scarlet panties, and the sheathed Kevlar knife that was strapped to her thigh.

Donny blushed, and they all burst out laughing.

"Seriously." Karmelian said. "You are both armed, I hope? This evening could be tricky if we are recognised."

Donny said, "I'm carrying....." Abby broke in with an impish grin. "And so am I." She lifted her skirt with a flourish exhibiting a similar knife to Karla's strapped to her equally graceful thigh, though the panties this time were white.

When they all settled down again, Jennock who had done a second circuit around the block to give them time to get over the hilarity, deposited them at the doors to the Paris casino, and drove off.

The evening went off well. They dined, played a little blackjack and roulette, caught a glimpse of their quarry, and left the casino to foregather in the suite at 'Circus, Circus', occupied by Karmelian, Karla and Jennock.

Abby asked the question that Donny hesitated to ask. "What happened to Pirello and his people?

Jennock answered. "We discussed killing them. Then we decided to frame them instead. My friend at the Las Vegas police department knew them well, but he had trouble pinning anything on them. So we fixed them up with burglary tools and broke into the back of one of the desert gambling joints with a brothel on the side. My guy was waiting with some friends. As soon as we got the bunch inside the woman started screaming rape. The cops came in and didn't see us at all, but they saw Pirello and his man and the screaming woman. They grabbed them and read them their rights. Pirello was pointing at us screaming it was a frame. The cops ignored him, told him to shut up and cuffed him. When he pointed at us, the cops said there was no one there. They must be on drugs. They were of course and there was extra in their pockets, enough to add trafficking to the list of charges. Pirello and his man will do big time, the woman a slap on the wrist. She turned state's evidence and gave them up, admitting they had been discussing robbing the joint to make a big drug buy. She kept her mouth shut about the party earlier."

Karmelian turned to Donny. "We would have probably dropped them into the river, but we realized that if you found out there would be a problem. So this way we do the police a favor *and* get rid of some rubbish." He gave a thin smile. "It would still have been easier perhaps, if we had buried them in the desert."

Taking suitable precautions, the new allies watched the progress of the Regret camp. But it was obvious that the only way anything was going to happen was if they initiated the action.

Then Charles Regret left Las Vegas.

Chapter nine

It was a complete surprise and they only discovered it when Karla got talking with one of the housemaids at the Paris Hotel. She had cultivated many of the staff on the pretence of looking for a job. As a result she was regarded as one of them. The story came out that Regret had upset the management and he was evicted. All very discretely of course, but she had overheard her boss arguing with Regret about news he had received that there were enquiries being made by Treasury agents. Regret was being sought for interview.

Elsewhere, Homeland Security was picking up the links between suspected payments being used for large arms shipments between East and West, especially links that pointed toward Pakistan and Afghanistan, all linked to the private bank that Regret had been running for the past several years.

It meant that Charles Regret decided that a sojourn elsewhere would be sensible. He departed in a private jet the same day.

Large sums of money had been deposited for the removal of the people named by Regret.

The money was payable only after the public announcement of their deaths. The identity was expected to be verified by fingerprint or DNA, otherwise no pay.

The rewards offered made the continuing stay of the group in Las Vegas a pointless risk. Having decided to move, they made immediate preparations. Since all were on the list and involved, they decided to set out initially together. It was Karmelian who pointed out that the desert around the city was the ideal place for an ambush. In the circumstances staying together for the desert stretch made sense. The five-strong party left in two cars. Donny replaced the Galaxy with a convertible. The others acquired a stretch-cab Ford pickup.

Arnold Warner was pissed-off big time. He turned to his companion who shared the front seat of the truck. "Pass me another beer, for Pete's sake. This is becoming a complete pain in the ass."

His companion, Chip Peters, shrugged. "The boss says we do this, we do this!"

"They will just board a plane to blow Vegas. Why would they bother to drive?"

"Boss said cover all angles, so what's the beef. We got nothing else to do. If they come this way we block the road while the others do the business. We don't even have to raise a sweat."

The dawn light appeared before the call came. "Arnie, we got trade coming your way, a green convertible two passengers." The caller had not realized that the pick-up that preceded the convertible was driven by the other named fugitives. "We are following the convertible, hanging back, but well in sight, there are no other cars between us. There is a pick-up ahead of the convertible, so let it through before you block. Have you got that?"

"Yeah, I got it."

The pick-up appeared in the distance, and after a few heart-stopping moments the truck engine caught and fired up.

Jennock, driving saw the truck as he passed and it puzzled him. He shook Karmelian. The truck had pulled out across the road. Jennock stopped. Karmelian said, "Ambush!"

Jennock reversed and spun the pick-up, driving back to the truck.

Both Arnie and Chip were watching the approaching convertible. They could see the chase Galaxy in the distance closing fast. The pick-up coasted to a stop and all three occupants got out, Karmelian carrying a rifle, Jennock a shotgun and Karla a long-barrelled handgun.

In the truck Arnie noticed the pick-up and shouted to Chip, "We got company." He pulled his gun and searched around for the occupants. Realizing that they must have passed round to the other side of the vehicle, he was not surprised when the door on the other side of the cab was snatched open, he fired two shots through the open door. Chip was unluckily in the path of the answering shot that came from Jennock's shot-gun. He toppled without a sound out of the door revealing the shotgun-carrying Jennock.

"Out!" Jennock wagged the gun sugges-tively. Arnie held out and dropped his 9mm automatic, and slid out of the cab. The Galaxy had arrived. Six men tumbled out guns in hand. Donny and Abby both exited the convertible, weapons ready, as soon as they realised they had been blocked.

The first man out of the Galaxy dropped his Ingram SMG, clattering as it hit the tarmac of the road surface. He was dead when he hit the ground. The others all made it and scattered to the roadside ditches for cover. They immediately started shooting at the now dispersed group of allies.

The boom of the shotgun brought a yelp from one of the attackers as he was brushed by the edge of the spread of the pellets. He suffered a single bloody wound down his arm. It did not incapacitate him but it did infuriate him. He sent a storm of bullets from the mini-gun he held, the bullets scattered over a wide area doing no damage but venting his feelings anyway.

His boss yelled at him to stop wasting shells and keep his head down.

He reloaded the gun and cocked it. Unfortunately he neglected to watch while he did so. Jennock had moved in the meantime, and his next shot finished what the first had started. The mini-gun dropped, fully loaded and cocked, ready for action, from the dead hand of its owner.

The second car arrived with reinforcements. Their ambushers had not anticipated running into a gun battle with experienced opponents. They exited their car carefully, dropping swiftly into the ditches guns up and ready.

Donny started to move forward. As he moved a shooter lifted up a little to get a clear shot at the moving man. Abby shot him twice in the head before he dropped back into the ditch, casualty number four. The remaining attackers found themselves having to keep heads down, in peril of having them blown off.

Danny called to Abby, "Can one of you move the truck, another take the car through then bring the truck back again?"

Karmelian, heard, "We got it. Are the keys on the car still with it?"

Abby answered, "Yes. It's all ready to go." She rose at that point and fired a burst from a captured Ingram at the ditch shielding three of the surviving attackers. She dropped into cover once more before anyone could target her.

Karmelian called to Jennock, "Can you handle the truck?"

The laconic voice from further down the ditch answered. "I got it."

Karla called softly, "I've got the car."

Donny, Abby and Karmelian took the cue and all rose and started blazing away at the positions of the surviving attackers, whose enthusiasm was at a low ebb by this time.

While the heads were down, the truck started up and moved back out of the way of the car which ghosted forward under Karla's control. Once it passed, Jennock pulled the truck forward, blocking the road once more. He parked and took the keys with him when he dropped out of the door. Still firing in turns the other three backed up to the truck and jumped into their vehicles setting off at high speed down the road to Los Angeles.

Karmelian called Abby on his cell phone. "Abby, tell Donny to pull ahead of us. If we are followed we'll run interference. but I don't really expect it. We will be splitting at Barstow. We decided that we would try 'Frisco. Enjoy LA, watch your backs and keep in touch, kids." He broke the contact and Donny overtook the pick-up with a wave, leaving it gradually dropping further behind in the distance.

Abby turned to Donny. "How about that? He started off hunting us down. Now we are old friends."

Donny grinned. "Sharing a shower of bullets can have that effect, or hadn't you noticed?"

Abby laughed. "When you put that way it makes sense."

The rest of the journey to Los Angeles was uneventful and the two young people soon found accommodation in a Ramada hotel, on West Olympic Blvd.

The sight of Abby in a bikini beside the pool was enough to keep Donny occupied. Despite having seen her many times before in various stages of dress, the bikini never failed to thrill. There were other women around the pool, but he only had eyes for Abby. She walked around the poolside with her towel draped over her shoulder, completely unconscious of the effect she was having. At least it looked as if she was. When she arrived she said breathlessly to Donny,

"I felt I was being stripped by the men as I walked round here."

Donny looked at the people seated about the pool edges. "It's the penalty for being the best-looking woman in the area. I think I could rent you out quite easily here. What do you think?"

As Abby punched him in the arm, he laughed and she giggled, despite herself. "What do you think I would fetch?" She whispered.

"Twenty bucks, easy," he whispered back.

They both collapsed laughing, raising several eyebrows around the pool.

For three days they enjoyed LA and Hollywood, doing all the things visitors have done ever since the movies came to Beverly Hills. It was in the evening of the fourth day that they spotted Regret. He was in company with several of the well-dressed socialite set and they were all tumbling into a night club, in a group.

Donny and Abby were passing in the convertible at the time. Immediately the joy of the evening drive past the beautiful people lost its flavor. They drove back to the hotel. Abby called Karmelian to let him know. They knew he wished to conclude his arrangement with the one-time banker.

The re-union occurred the following day when the other three turned up at the hotel, filing in turn through the door of the three-bedroom suite they had transferred to, due to the circumstances.

First came Karmelian, who grinned and kissed Abby on the cheek as he came in, then Karla who kissed Donny on the cheek, also smiling. Jennock came in looking dead-pan as if he couldn't be bothered with all this nonsense. After they had sorted themselves out in the other two rooms, they sat sprawled around the lounge area with drinks and snacks provided by room service.

Karla stretched, looking sideways at Donny as she did so, trying to see if he got the full effect of the toned body. She was disappointed as Donny was deep in conversation with Karmelian.

Jennock spoke. "Regret is planning a trip on his boat down to Catalina Island and maybe on to San Diego or probably Mexico. He is not making it public, but he has tipped off a few people he wants as guests. I understand, among them will be Archie Monaghan, the man they call the Magician."

Karmelian shook his head. "He is headed for the hills in that case." He explained! "Archie is the man you call when you want your money to disappear from everyone's view but your own. He is credited with hiding, not laundering, actually hiding the location of billions of unlaundered funds for the Mob by the CIA. You name them, he has worked for them. When he gets control of your funds, they disappear, they reappear, short his usual fee of course, on demand for the key holder only. No names, just codes!"

Regret is definitely dropping out of sight."

He sat back looking thoughtful.

Donny picked up his Satphone, pressed a speed dial and waited. A voice answered, he spoke. Archie Monaghan, interested?"

Jonathon at the other end said, "Where did he come in?"

Donny repeated, "Interested or not?"

Jonathon caught the impatient note in Donny's voice. "Yes, interested."

"We need a boat here in Los Angeles, seagoing motor or sail, six-berth at least. Regret is here and is on the run. He has the Magician lined up to go with him. Regret may not survive the trauma yet to occur. Would a captive magician be of interest? The collateral damage may be considerable as the people after Regret are extremely pissed off with him. Unpaid bills and such, plus the odd attempt to clear the slate with a burp gun, if you take my meaning."

"How long for? What about crew?"

"One month, max. There are five of us, and any crew better be bullet-proof."

"I see. Leave it with me. I'll be back to you quickly. First, where are you? When is the deadline for the boat?"

"Los Angeles, and 12 hours from now. Can you do it?"

"Consider it done. But you are costing me favors."

"Just think of all those corners we have cleared out for you during the last couple of years. They have to be worth a few favors surely." Donny was well aware that the organization that Jonathon worked for had gained considerable kudos for the sub-rosa activities involving Abby and himself since the first incident in the channel two years ago.

He switched the phone off and turned to the others. "We should have a boat by later tonight. Can we get a watch on Regret?"

Jennock said, "There is already. Gentleman Roger Hamilton, the bookie, has his boys on the job. Willie Jo Manner has someone out. I'm not sure who. And I hear that Emilio Grimaldi is asking around about some money which was not credited to his account at Regret's former place of employment. I guess that is the reason that Regret is leaving in a hurry. Emilio's Casino group control half the gambling in Las Vegas, and considerable real-estate in Los Angeles. Emilio has a reputation for fitting people, whom he thinks have crossed him, with concrete boots and dropping them in the river."

"Where," asked Karla, "does he find a river to drop them at Las Vegas?"

"To Emilio, it doesn't matter. His father and grandfather did it. So he keeps up the tradition. So the river is dry. The victims are going nowhere from the riverbed, not with well-fitted concrete boots. So it takes longer and they die of sunburn or something, as long as they die anyway. That's all Emilio is concerned with." Jennock sounded almost sympathetic as he mentioned the fate of some of these victims.

Karmelian nodded and added, "He is also a vindictive s.o.b, and will spend well over the odds to get back at someone he thinks has cheated or insulted him. I always thought that to him, cheating and insulting were the same thing when they were applied to dealings with his organization. Wake me when something happens. He shook his head at Karla, went into the room they were sharing and lay down. He was asleep in seconds.

The others sprawled around the lounge for a while, then headed for their rooms to rest while waiting for Jonathon to call back.

Abby stirred at the sound of the Satphone bleep. She lifted Donny's arm from its comfortable location over her body, and stretched out for the beeping instrument.

"Yes, Jonathon? What have you got for us?"

"Hi, Abby. I have a 60-ft' Naval Patrol boat conversion named *Isis*. Now charters as a cruising yacht out of St Catalina Island. It is fully provisioned for eight and will be alongside on the Carnival Cruises Quay beside the Queen Mary by 2300 tonight. The skipper and engineer go with the boat; both are ex-navy Seals. Both are prepared for whatever might happen. Abby! They are contracted to you and Donny only. Do you understand?"

"Yes Jonathon. Weapons?"

"Code ATLAS, the locker under the settee berth in the lounge–port side. The skipper is Pete Morrow and he will back you to the limit."

Donny had aroused himself and was sharing the Satphone with a trailing headset. "Hi, Jonathon. Are you saying that this Pete Morrow is one of ours?"

"He is a privateer on retainer; over several years has proved reliable. Good luck, please do not start World War Three."

The tall lines of one of the icons of the beautiful life were outlined against the skyline of her Long Beach Mooring. Jennock slid the convertible into the employee's car park behind the Carnival building.

They all piled out and Jennock placed the keys in the exhaust pipe for the rental rep to pick up, and followed the others out to the pier, untenanted at present by any cruise ships. As they approached the Cruise Line dock, the lights of the boat secured alongside became visible.

A voice called out as they approached, "Donny? Abby?"

Donny replied "*Isis*?"

"Welcome aboard. Soon as you like. We are not actually welcome here."

The party dropped down to the rising and falling boat, and as soon as the last boarder, Abby, landed on deck, the bow mooring was cast off and the boat swung out into the current that swiftly pulled it round into the direction of the open sea. The stern rope was released and the engines that had been muttering quietly opened up with a roar. The stern dug into the river waters and the boat lifted onto the plane and fled down river and out into the bay.

Isis rocked gently in the longer swells coming from deep sea. The entire group sat in the open lounge to the rear of the craft. Pete Morrow joined them leaving his crewman, Billy McCann, handling the engine controls and keeping watch on the bridge.

Donny introduced the group to Pete and pointed out that he was aware of the situation. He then asked Pete what was happening regarding Regret's boat.

"The boat is called *Risk*. She is steel, 120' twin diesels, complete with helipad and two tenders, both high speed launches." He lifted a remote control and pressed buttons. A 40-inch plasma screen arose from its location beside the forward bulkhead. On it appeared the radar picture of Los Angeles harbor and river mouth.

"This is the real-time picture of the local area." Pete picked up a laser designator and switched on. With the red spot he indicated a moving point crossing from the river into the bay heading toward St Catalina Island. "This is the *Risk*, Regret's yacht." He moved the pointer to another moving blip. "This is the *Double-Bet* belonging to Emilio Grimaldi, as you can see, it is keeping its distance from Regret's yacht, but I believe following it nonetheless.

"The *Double-Bet* is a 180' steel-hulled yacht fitted into the hull of a coastguard cutter. She is fast and believed to be well armed. The specification includes, apart from the usual package of helicopter, tenders etc., some fairly heavy weaponry."

He paused and looked around, checking that the group were following his dissertation. Satisfied he carried on. "Now we have this!" The pointer moved to another dot on the screen that appeared to be idly moving around in the bay area. "That is the drug distributor for the bay area. His name is Carmine Schultz. They say his father made a mistake with an Italian teacher, whose father had a bigger shotgun than his. So he married her in time to name the boy, and left soon afterward. Despite his mother's best efforts Carmine reverted to type and joined the drug set early. Took to it big time and, as you can guess, clawed his way up to a point where he needed the services of the money laundry. Like many others he has suddenly found a gap in his receipts, caused by the absconding Regret and the intervention of the bank inspectors.

"His boat is probably the fastest, apart from this one, and there will possibly be another that we have not yet seen. That will be for Gentleman Roger Hamilton. He is an unknown quantity in this game. If I was worried about anything, it would be the Gentleman. He's new on the scene and no one really has any idea what he can or will do. They don't even know if he will be involved in something like this. I do know that he is ex-Special Forces, probably Russian. Do not be deceived by the name. In Vegas names are as transient as fame.

"He did have his people keeping Regret under surveillance. His employees are also all ex-Special Forces from both sides of the Atlantic. That has been another worry for the local scene.

"That's it folks. It's up to you."

Pete sat back and waited for the next move.

Billy McCann poked his head through the door and with a mock Irish accent said. "Skipper-boss, the stew is ready to serve and the chef is getting desperate with the waiting!"

"In that case we can't have the chef put out. Everybody, let's eat." He got to his feet and walked through to the dining saloon, where the big saucepan of stew sent steam into the air. Next to it was a big mound of mashed potato, broccoli, and carrots, and a stack of plates. Everyone helped themselves and while they ate the whole chase was forgotten. Abby looked around the saloon. You would never guess the reason for this gathering from what she saw. It looked like a gathering at a local social club rather than a group proposing to lay heavy hands on a big time crook.

Chapter ten

The position of the blips on the radar had altered while the party ate. The major change was in the position of the drug boat. It was now rapidly gaining on the *Double-Bet*.

The whole group watched with interest as the two blips closed.

From the bridge, Billy called, "Fireworks started, sounds like a big .50 cal."

There was a loud bang. A flash of yellow flame outlined a low profile boat against the high sides of the casino owner's yacht.

"Carmine's boat is attacking the *Double-Bet*." Billy was sounding excited, so they all went up to the bridge to see what was going on.

It was obvious that there was a minor war going on between the two craft. There was certainly considerable volume of fire coming from the bigger craft. The .50 cal on the smaller boat was silent though there were still grenade rounds being exchanged at regular intervals. A searing, bright white shaft of light indicated a missile being fired from the drug smuggler. The high sides of the Casino yacht provided a target that couldn't be missed. The missile obviously penetrated the steel plates and hit something important because the *Double-Bet* slowed down and stopped, rocking, dead in the water. The flames were being reduced as the crew and the fire suppression system took effect. The gunfire from the stopped ship did not stop as the fighting men continued to pour their bullets into the smaller craft owned by the drug runners.

Donny turned to Pete. "How far has Regret managed to get while all this has been going on?"

Pete turned to the bridge repeater screen, checking on the location of all the boats concerned. "Well! Surprise, surprise. Guess who is way ahead of the fleet. Just one other boat in pursuit. I would think that would be Gentleman Roger. He obviously let the other two clear the way for him. My guess is that Regret will not suspect the latest arrival on the scene, but that doesn't mean that he will ignore it. I would guess he will clear the islands. If the new boat is near he will deal with it accordingly."

Abby looked at him keenly. "We, of course, are already out here ahead of Regret. You don't miss much do you, Pete?"

"I prefer to stay one step ahead if I can." Pete grinned. He shouted to Billy. "Wind her up. It's time we moved along to clear the island."

The mutter of the engines increased to a roar as Billy fed power to the big turbo-diesels. The *Isis* got under way once more. By continuing west out to St Nicholas Island, they managed to bring the *Risk* into sight as they came through the channel between Santa Catalina and San Clemente, giving the impression of travelling down coast from further north, perhaps San Francisco. As Peter pointed out the low profile of his boat presented a poor radar image on yacht radar. Since he was not squawking an identity signal, it would require physical sight to identify the *Isis.*

Karmelian, Jennock and Danny, were reviewing the armory. On the table in the saloon was an assembly of weaponry which, Abby decided, was sufficient to take on a company of soldiers at least. The grenade launchers fascinated her particularly. The chunky feel of the over and under-slung barrels, the 7.25mm upper and the much larger bore grenade launcher had a sort of comfortable feel when held ready for operation. The relative accuracy of the placing of a grenade round was impressive, and the much greater accuracy of the rifled barrel made it a highly versatile weapon. In the open weapons locker she could see the racked shoulder launcher for missiles stored separately at the far end of the locker. Two Colt bull-pups were clipped to the upturned lid and out on the table was an assortment of hand guns of various types, including the mini version of the Ingram and a Russian Makarov with an extended stick magazine. Abby pulled out her Walther PPK and extracted the magazine, not forgetting to eject the round in the chamber. Seating herself she picked up the cleaning gear and a pair of cotton gloves, and proceeded to strip the automatic and clean all the components before reassembling it. She unloaded the magazine clip and carefully wiped all the cartridges before replacing them. Satisfied, she inserted the magazine and loaded one round into the chamber. Removing the clip she replaced the missing cartridge and inserted it into place before setting the safety catch and replacing the weapon in her belt holster. The others looked on with interest at the performance.

When Donny came down and went through the same routine, Jennock nodded approvingly. It was something that he could relate to. Warriors looked after their weapons. At least real warriors do, and this confirmed the impression he had formed already of the two young Britons.

"So what is the plan? As far as Abby and I are concerned, we will be happy to get Regret off our case. And that would be enough. I realize that you all have something else in mind. Neither

Abby nor I have any intention of leaving it all to you. So where do we go from here?"

Karmelian shrugged. "Apart from the survival bit, Regret owes us all a lot of money for work undertaken. He is so rich it is difficult to understand why he didn't just pay the bills and send us off. It would have been the simplest way. Thinking about it, if he still wanted to dispose of us, it would have been much easier in those circumstances as we would have been unaware. Trying to kill us over the past weeks was a big mistake. I would like to confirm that for him as soon as possible. I guess he paid Carmine Schultz to stop Grimaldi. I think by being out already before he left port we are probably below his horizon at the moment. If he decides to stop overnight, I propose to attack tonight. We will need to get aboard unseen and unheard. He has plenty of ways to run given notice, so whatever we do has to be real quiet." Jennock said, "There is a half deck at the stern where the cooks dump the kitchen scraps, it could be a good way in."

Pete came in carrying a roll of charts. "This might be of interest to you if you are planning a visit to the gin palace…The *Risk.*"

He unrolled the charts and revealed a schematic of the plans of a big ocean-going cruiser. "These are the working drawings. I was able to get the copies from the Registry with a little help from my friends!" He jangled a bunch of innocent looking keys as he spoke. Before going any further he turned to Donny and Abby. "This okay with you two?"

Donny nodded, "We are in and looking forward to rearranging Mr Regret's future. He has been seriously intrusive into our affairs ever since we landed in USA. This included several attempts to kill us. Abby and I are murder intolerant, specifically our murders, and that of our friends. Stopping Charles Regret has become a priority."

"Right, then let's take a look at what we got here." Pete put weights on the corners of the drawings and then explained what they were seeing in layman's terms.

"That half deck you mentioned, Jennock, is here and the doors connect to the galley as well as the main service corridor. The craft is built like a cruise ship on a smaller scale, and it requires a crew of eighteen. The crew are all trained seamen and women. None of them is part of the protection that Regret has 24/7. They are the extra people who are accommodated in the mid-section on the deck between the engine room and the bridge.

"He carries six in his protection squad. On this trip he has eight. They work in pairs, never less than two on duty at any one time."

Donny looked at him sharply at this point.

Pete forestalled the question holding up his hand. "I am a professional charter skipper, I know all of the other pro's in the area. Bill Williams, skipper of *Risk,* and I get together regularly. We all talk about charters and clients, and the fact that Regret has recently dropped into view, having, in the past only used the yacht for entertaining on a few occasions. The sudden requirement for a voyage created a rise in interest, and the increase in personnel was a topic for discussion between friends. Where are they headed? You may well ask. Only Regret knows at present. When he makes up his mind, I will be informed.

"It is pretty obvious, since no attempt to load heavy ordinance was made, that he is depending on others to protect him with heavy weaponry. Carmine Schultz was one level of protection. How about Gentleman Roger Hamilton's boat currently in trail, as another?"

The presence of the *Snark,* Hamilton's boat, was a complication they had not entirely made provision for.

As it happened the problem solved itself. The *Snark* went alongside the *Risk* and three men boarded through the accommodation door in the side of the yacht. Then it dropped back and reversed its course, heading back to Los Angeles.

The *Risk,* now behind San Clemente Island, dropped anchor in the lee of the island out of sight and off the radar to any but the most specific searcher. The *Isis* stopped out of sight of the other craft, though still within easy range. The bay where they anchored was used on a regular basis by fishermen, though the season was advanced and there were no other boats present at the time.

With the dropping of the anchor, preparation began immediately for an excursion to the *Risk* anchored the other side of the point. The two ribs were in the water, the electric outboards tested and installed. All the party were outfitted in black coveralls especially developed for the use of Special Operations forces. The double skin of the coveralls was lined with thin sheets of Kevlar that could flex and allow easy movement without noise. There was even a hood with similar protection that could fold down and be held in place by Velcro stip.

The various pockets and sheaths were built-in, and accommodated the smaller hand weapons carried by the team.

The team lowered themselves into the two ribs, settling themselves around the seats. Pete joined them similarly dressed. "You don't expect me to trust you with my super suits without at least coming to protect my investment." He was carrying a missile launcher and a bag containing two reloads. Strapped to his shoulder was one of the Bull-pups, with a bandolier draped across his chest.

Leaving Billy in charge the two ribs ghosted out to sea to clear the point.

The *Risk* was anchored in the shelter of the headland and the lights made her appear to be sitting in a pool of gold. Both ribs went for the stern gallery, the quiet motors hardly a mutter, lost in the sounds of the waves on the shore. The padded grapnel caught the rail of the stern gallery. The rib was attached alongside, the painter hooked to a magnet clamped firmly to the steel hull. The second rib arrived and hooked on with its own grapnel, and magnet. All the raiders climbed up onto the gallery where they split up and disappeared into the yacht.

Donny and Abby worked as a team. Pete came with them. They took the port side corridor. The other three took starboard.

On their soft-soled shoes the two groups drifted their separate ways through the working deck of the anchored ship. Between them the teams gathered the crew members off watch, binding and gagging them as they cleared the lower deck. Most of the men and women of the crew were from Mexico, the others from the

Philippines. The two groups met in the crew common room in the bows of the yacht, and compared notes. Nowhere had they encountered any resistance. They had collected the entire crew according to Pete's records.

None of the protection squad on board had been encountered. So they presumed they were all in the deck accommodation where the saloon and bar were situated.

The serving staff verified that the owner and his friends were in the deck saloon area.

Karla and Abby selected two of the waitresses—more or less their sizes—and took them through to one of the other cabins, returning shortly dressed in the smart outfits worn by the female staff. None of the men could do the same because all of them were far too big to squeeze into the male staff clothes.

Jennock grinned when he saw the uniforms. "I could never resist a woman in a uniform." Both women smiled and did a twirl for the benefit of their companions.

"Will we do?" Abby asked.

"You'll do for me," Donny said giving her a hug.

Karla said, "Hair!" She flung a dark wig over to Abby. Both women stood in front of the wall mirror and gathered their own hair under a net before fitting the dark wigs in place. The difference made was startling. Karla went to work on Abby's fair complexion with a brush and cosmetics, giving her a sallow look that accorded with the complexions of the waitresses they were replacing. She had just completed her own make-up when the buzzer went summoning service from the saloon. Collecting a tray, Karla left the room followed discreetly by Abby, Pete and Karmelian. The call was from the protection squad, lounging around the saloon. The figure of Regret and Gentleman Roger could be seen through the glass doors, in the bar and snug area. None of the protection crew took much notice of Karla as she took their orders for drinks and snacks. There were only eight men there at the time. When she came below to fill the orders she passed on the news to the others, and left them trying to work out where the other two men were. Finally deciding that they had to be with the ship's officers, Pete took Jennock exploring to find them before they could become an embarrassment.

The bridge of the *Risk* was what could be expected of a yacht of this size and quality. Roomy and packed with electronics in addition to an old-fashioned ships wheel for the owners to play at helmsman. Connected electronically to the steering, it was in effect a computer game rather than the real thing. To the rear was the captain's sea cabin. In fact it was where he spent most of his time at sea. Pete and Jennock found the first missing man, wandering back and forth across the bridge, humming quietly to himself.

From the sea cabin came another voice. Jennock described it as 'irritated Brooklyn'.

"For Pete's sake, find another tune to hum. That's driving me nuts!"

"Fuck off, Toyboy. Go play with your dolls." The man replied continued his strolling and humming.

Jennock and Pete looked at each other. Pete nodded to the sea cabin and Jennock pointed to the stroller. Taking his knife from its leg sheath he waited until the man turned to return across the bridge, rose behind him without a sound and slipped the knife into the side of the man's neck as his hand covered his mouth. A twist of the blade severed the spinal cord.

As he lowered the body to the deck Jennock took up the humming remembering to keep the same annoying tune that had upset the man's companion in the sea cabin.

Pete meanwhile had slipped over to the door of the sea cabin and took a quick peek inside. Four men were seated on the floor. All were tied and gagged. The Captain saw and recognised Pete, apart from widening his eyes he made no other sign. He flicked his eyes to his left and Pete was able to glimpse their guard sitting on the berth, with a pack of cards in front of him. The silenced automatic popped as the man's eyes opened wide at the sight of the gun. He collapsed forward over the cards. Pete checked his pulse. There was none. Pulling the body upright, he made sure the man was not wearing a Kevlar vest. Satisfied he let the man fall once more and turned to the Skipper. Holding his finger up to his lips, he indicated downwards, then he held his hand up with five fingers spread, indicating back in five minutes, and turned and left the tied and gagged men.

The pair went below to rejoin the group.

Pete explained the situation to the others. The crew were all secure, and with the location of all the others now established it seemed that they had covered all the angles.

The group split into their two sections once more. Donny, Abby and Pete made their way to the protection group still lounging in the next room to the saloon.

It took a few seconds for the bodyguards to realize that they had been infiltrated. By then it was too late. In the other room through the glass they saw the entry of Karla followed by Karmelian and Jennock. Seeing the two men being secured Pete opened the door between them. All the men present were disarmed and secured with plastic handcuffs.

Karmelian turned to Gentleman Roger. "How much did he offer you to join forces?"

Roger Hamilton was cool and after a moment he shrugged and said, "$5 mil. We were just deciding where and how it would be paid."

Jennock sneered. "You obviously were not aware that Charles Regret pays off in lead, not gold or dollars. You're a gambler. What odds would you give me that Carmine Schultz is not on his way now to close the account with you?"

Gentleman Roger looked up at the bland face of Charles Regret. He saw nothing there to verify or deny the charge. His own face showed nothing. He shrugged once more and sank back on the cushions of his seat and waited for whatever came next.

Turning to Regret Karmelian said, "Let us open your safe and see just what we have here." He waved the gun at the end wall of the saloon.

Regret shook his head. "I don't think so."

The silenced shot made very little noise. Shocked, Regret looked at his left foot. The designer shoe now had a neat hole in it. Blood leaked out staining the expensive carpeting.

"Where were we now? Oh, yes. The safe, please?"

For a moment Regret looked as if he would refuse once more. Karmelian casually swung his gun toward Regret's right foot.

"No...no. I'll open the safe." He said hastily, and started hopping over to the rear wall of the saloon.

Pete's radio vibrated and he pressed the receive button. Billy's voice came over the air. "Company is coming boss. Looks like Carmine is buying in."

Chapter eleven

Pete thought for a moment. "Sink him!" He said eventually.

"Wow. Can I?" Without waiting for confirmation Billy switched off. From behind the point the sound of engines throttling up came before the *Isis* swept round the point at speed and joined them in the bay. From over the headland the noise of a power boat approaching was interrupted by a twanging noise. The propellers on the boat stopped suddenly. The engine screamed and the explosion that followed was accompanied by a corona of fire that rose above the ridge of the headland.

"The safe!" Karmelian reminded Regret, "Open please."

A button in the frame of the huge plasma screen caused the entire section to sink out of the way. The vault door disclosed looked formidable. Regret pressed buttons on a keypad and the door opened slowly. It revealed a series of shelves stacked with packets of banknotes. At a sign from Karmelian, Regret started removing and stacking the plastic packets of banknotes on the table. The amount on view totalled four million by the time he finished stacking.

Donny watched all this and then stepped out of the saloon noting the depth of the wall where the safe was situated. The cabin forward of the saloon had a rear wall that left a deep space, at least four feet unaccounted for.

Returning to the saloon he went over to the open safe and examined the nest of pigeon holes carefully. Finding an upright that moved slightly, he pushed it to one side. Then he stood back and watched the look of horror which crossed the face of Charles Regret. The section of pigeon holes had collapsed and the back wall separated to reveal the other half of the safe stacked with even more packs of bills, piled around a central box. Pete stepped in and removed it. He unclipped the front panel and it revealed a set of trays containing matched gem stones in neat rows. There was a collective gasp from the watchers as the light caught the multi-coloured rows of stones. The effect was breathtaking.

Karmelian said, "Ah that is really something. I think in the circumstances we will be able to settle our accounts at least." He looked across at Jennock. "What do you say?" Jennock looked in turn at Karla, raising his right eyebrow.

"Payday!" was Karla's comment. "And I guess there might be enough to see the kids through college too." She looked in turn at Donny and Abby.

The cash total had risen to twelve million. No one had any idea what the gems would fetch. Pete went up to the bridge and released the Captain and other officers. He told them where to find the crew. He also warned them that they would be lucky to get paid as the boss only had the yacht and its contents left. All his money was now gone.

The Captain looked at Pete strangely, then led him through the bridge deck to the cabin that occupied the same place only on the other side of the ship, as his own sea cabin. Opening the door with a key from his own key ring, he showed Pete the safe concealed behind the panel beneath the berth. "I cannot promise that there is anything there, but I did see him in here with a big crate. It never came out as far as I know."

He bent down in front of the safe and started to twist the dial. "This boat is on lease, we were paid up front for a three month voyage. Ten grand would see the crew happy with close mouths."

The safe door swung open and ten gold bars clinked onto the floor as the yacht rocked to a swell. Twenty bars had been packed into the safe. There was room for no more. Pete stood up. "Now let us look at the safe in your sea cabin."

For a moment it looked as if the Captain might protest. Then he shrugged. "Let's see what there is in there."

Not surprisingly the safe in the Captain's cabin divulged another collection of gold bars. According to Pete's quick calculation about two million dollars approximately between the two safes.

Regret's face fell when he realized that the gold had been found. When the Captain walked in, his face hardened, guessing that he had revealed the location of the gold.

"And now what comes next?" he addressed Karmelian.

Karmelian smiled. "If it were up to me I would tie a loop round your ankle and tow you along behind the yacht for as long as it took for the sharks to feed. As it is, it is not up to me. Donny and Abby are in charge of this little party."

Charles Regret looked at him in disbelief. "The kids?"

"Planned the whole operation, having captured Jennock, Karla and me. They recruited us, and here we are face to face once more. This time in a position to receive our payment as promised. Planned and carried out by Donny and Abby. You really should have guessed they were no pushover after attempting to dispose of them over the past weeks."

"What will it cost me to get out of here?"

Donny joined the conversation. "Indulge me. You were going to cruise down the Baja coast to a nice deserted spot. There you intended taking a boat for a picnic ashore, with one or two of your bodyguards. While you were there a terrible accident would occur on the yacht, which would blow up with all hands and guests aboard.

"Tragic phone calls for help frantic search for survivors, regretfully none found. All followed by a quiet withdrawal from the scene with retirement in private villa on private island. Happy ever after? Did I cover everything?"

He turned to Gentleman Roger. "Sorry, Roger. You didn't make it."

The mask cracked and Roger turned to Charles Regret. "That was a mistake. Why do I suspect that the boat is probably ready to go now? Everything in place for the swift getaway."

Abby strolled out onto the deck and wandered along to the two power boats sitting side by side forward. Both were fitted with canvas covers neatly lashed down.

Abby called Jennock. He came out on deck and joined her. While she stood back covering him, he unhooked the rope tied to the deck cleat.

The taut canvas slackened. Jennock unhooked it and threw it over the cabin of the cruiser. There was no sign of movement from within the boat. Jennock climbed aboard and checked the cabin and the lockers. Apart from safety equipment there was nothing there that should not have been there.

They went through the same performance with the other boat. Once more there was nothing unusual to be found.

Jennock remembered. "What about the boat used by Gentleman Roger? That is alongside at the moment."

Abby turned and looked over the side. Sure enough, there it was; 45ft of power boat, the dark painted cabin roof glinting in the light from some of the port holes.

The companionway was lowered already, so the two searchers descended the stairs and boarded. Regret's manservant was in the boat waiting.

"Show us around!" Abby suggested. The man gave them a tour of the boat. The galley was stocked fridge and freezers full The bar equally well stocked. The forward cabin was locked and there was no key available. Jennock produced a piece of pipe about twelve inches long and slipped it over the handle of the door. The lock was integrated with the handle, rather like the older hotels before the arrival of the keycards. With a sharp twist of the handle, the lock burst and the door sprang open. The entire bow cabin was stuffed with money and paper. The paper mostly bonds of various sorts, the money was vastly more than that found on the Yacht.

Abby used her cell. Donny answered. "Port side, the gentleman's power boat, stuffed with even more wealth."

"We will take that with us then. Anything else?"

"Regret's valet."

"Come on up. We will arrange things with Pete, the Captain and Karmelian. The final arrangement will I am sure please all the good guys. Though I think the bad men will be disappointed." His wry smile was evident as he turned back to the room and motioned Karmelian and Karla over.

The explanation took little time. The inferences from this new information were quickly drawn. The yacht must already be wired to explode.

Pete came through having spoken to the captain about the crew. All were regular employees of the charter company. Donny put him in the picture adding his own suggestion that the yacht was already rigged to blow, though no-one had any idea how or when it would happen. "So first of all, it will be insured, I guess?"

"Of course we are insured. But can we not find and defuse the explosives?"

"You are welcome to try, of course. But I have to point out that the explosives were placed at the order of Mr Regret who, I think, has demonstrated a complete disregard for human life and therefore has no doubt included several measures to make the dismantling of his works extremely difficult. Otherwise I suggest you stock the two boats and prepare to abandon ship."

Stunned, the captain's mouth opened and closed twice as he coped with the enormity of the disaster facing his crew as well as himself. He snapped out of it and spun round calling his officers to prepare the boats and warn the crew to collect their belongings ready to abandon ship.

By the time the gold and money had been transferred to the power boat and Pete's *Isis,* the captain and crew had transferred to the two ship's boats. Donny took two of the bundles of cash and gave them to the Captain before he sailed off, still worried, but happy to have the money to share out with his crew.

The people belonging to Regret's entourage were getting restless. Regret himself was calm once more and showed no particular interest in the welfare of his men. From this, Abby concluded that most of them, if not all, had been destined for the discard in some way. From his record so far, she expected that the discharge would have been finalized with a bullet.

All eight of the heavy mobsters were transferred to the beach. They faced the long walk to the other end of the island where help could be found. Regret and Gentleman Roger were still on board when the first of the charges went off. Karmelian raced down the accommodation ladder and leapt onto the power boat. "Take off. She is about to blow." He shouted. Jennock slashed the remaining mooring rope and Karla opened the throttles causing the power boat to surge forward with a huge turmoil of white water from the thrust of the big diesels.

The *Isis* had already stood off, its own cargo of gold and money loaded and Donny and Abby aboard. All of them gathered in the wheelhouse to watch the spectacular demise of the beautiful yacht. It took remarkably little time for the whole event to be over. The final sigh of the hot metal slipping under the waves, was less than thirty minutes from the first explosion.

Before they departed Donny spoke on the TBS to Karmelian on the power boat. "What did you do with Regret and Gentleman Roger?"

"Nothing, I did not have time. When the explosions began I just managed to make it to the boat myself, there was no time to go and fetch them from the saloon. I'm afraid they had to take their chances. We are looking, but I don't hold out much hope of finding them."

Half an hour later, Pete hauled a very battered Gentleman Roger out of the water. He was still alive, a miracle in itself. He recovered enough to say that he had left Regret in the saloon and made a run for it when the first explosion occurred. He had been stunned when one of the bigger explosions had gone off while he was swimming away from the sinking boat. He had somehow stayed afloat. He had no idea what had happened to Regret. Bluntly he didn't care. Whatever happened he had asked for it.

The return to LA was a subdued affair. No effort was made to advise the authorities of the true circumstances of the loss of the *Risk* and of Carmine Schulz's cruiser.

The captain from the *Risk* reported piracy and a miraculous escape when the pirates loaded their gear on board, having allowed the crew to move their things into the ships boats. He described graphically the explosions that he attributed to the stuff loaded aboard by the pirate crew. There were no survivors in the water though he did believe there had been some of the men ashore when disaster struck.

For the charter company, the insurance paid out and the *Risk* was replaced. There was little further news after the first flurry of publicity, and the matter was soon yesterday's news.

For Donny and Abby there was a struggle of conscience over the acceptance of their share of the loot from the Regret horde. Neither had any real problem with the portions taken by Karmelian, Jennock and Karla. All had been promised rewards that they were never expected to collect, so Regret's money was justified. The fact that the fees payable were for the removal of Donny and Abby now seemed immaterial.

Pete took his share on the basis that sticking his neck out justified a commensurate fee. On that basis he made it clear that in his opinion the British couple, having been harassed and hounded across the entire country, definitely qualified for reimbursement on at least the same scale.

When Abby decided at last to consult Jonathon on the subject, his response was positive and immediate. "Take it, you earned it. From what I hear you have rid the USA of a very significant villain. There is no way that the origin of the funds you receive can be traced. As a matter of interest, in your dealings with Charles Regret, did you come across any obscure references to numbers or codes?"

Abby said, "Sorry, Jonathon. We did very little of the actual contact with Regret himself. I will check with Donny. If there is anything we'll let you know."

She logged off and thought for a while. Then, having decided, she went to find Donny. He was looking at the heap of packets of bills and wondering how he could actually get them to a place where they could be looked after properly and made available for spending.

"Donny, have you still got Regret's cell phone?"

He looked at her blankly for a moment. "Why, yes. It's in my bag in the bedroom." They were staying in a rented apartment in Beverly Hills, having decided to make sure there were no loose ends to get in the way of their freedom when they decided to move on.

Abby found the bag and retrieved the cell phone. With it in her hand she turned to Donny. "Remember Karmelian said that Charles Regret had meetings with Archie Monaghan?"

"Yes. So what?"

"Let us see if there actually was any transaction involved that Regret kept record of."

She switched on the cell phone and checked the files. There did not seem to be any allusions in the files to the Magician. She started going through the other sections of the telephone record system. It was not until she started going through the list of saved phone numbers that they found what they were looking for.

It was an entry with the initials A,M only when she pressed the call button, another number appeared on the screen. A man's voice answered the phone. Abby passed the phone to Donny and when the man asked for the reference, he read off the number on the screen. The voice answered asking for an amount required.

"Please quote what balance is available." Donny sounded almost bored.

"One moment please!" A computer generated voice reeled off the amount available."

For a moment Donny was stunned. Then he said, "Please transfer ten million to Barclays International, Grand Cayman, opening a new account. Make available on Password only." He gave a carefully spelled password, and closed the call.

"What was the balance?" Abby asked.

"One hundred and twenty million dollars," Donny said quietly.

"And you transferred ten million to a new account at Barclays in the Cayman Islands?"

"It occurred to me initially that, if I pass the account over to Jonathon, his boss is going to acquire the lot and use it as he sees fit. Well, call me suspicious. I think there are other projects in this world that deserve money more than the international spy game. Do you disapprove?" He looked at Abby hopefully.

Abby hugged him. "I approve wholeheartedly. I am so proud of you. I presume you transferred the ten million in case we lost control of the other account."

"Exactly, I am now going to see what I can do to lose the other one hundred and twenty million." He pressed the AM code and when the voice answered, he ordered the opening of accounts in Switzerland, Luxembourg, Lichtenstein and Singapore. He left $100 in the AM system, distributing the balance of one hundred and twenty million between the new accounts, carefully noting the new passwords he designated for each account.

From the internet he garnered the telephone numbers of all the accounts he had just created. Two numbers he passed to Abby, with the relevant passwords. "Call, give the password. Check the balance and change the password." He looked her in the eye and watched as she realized what he was saying. Confident she understood the reason, he left her to it and went into the other room to work on his own list. The last call he made was to the Cayman bank, where he changed his password.

Abby confirmed her list had been verified and passed over the new passwords.

Their final problem was the disposal of the acquired wealth/compensation from their eventful transit of the United States. They solved the problem by bagging the loot and flying by charter to Grand Cayman, where an extremely helpful bank official took charge of their embarrassment of funds, making it disappear alarmingly swiftly into a series of smaller accounts before finishing up, after suitable charges had been taken back in the Password account, available for immediate use.

The urbane young man who arranged all this assured them that the interest paid on such a substantial sum would reimburse the charges taken within three days.

Chapter twelve

They took the regular flight from the islands to Miami. Spending a few days at the legendary city seemed like a good idea, so they checked in to one of the Art Deco hotels at the beach and spent the next few days chilling out. As Abby pointed out "Chilling out in Miami seems to be a contradiction in terms—but what the hell?"

The problem they were finding was that after the excitement and drama of the past weeks, it was difficult to settle down and relax. Inevitably they found after just a week, there was only so much beach time they could handle before the itch to move on became too much.

The Mercedes convertible ate up the coast highway at a steady fifty-five miles per hour, the breeze enough to keep both of them cool enough to enjoy the ride. The car at least let them feel they were moving on, going somewhere at least.

In fact they were just driving north with no established plan, happy to be alone together without the feeling of being trailed.

They made a stop at Orlando, destination of many of their friends back in England. They checked into a hotel there to do a tour of the various studio 'worlds'

The combination of crowds, queues and noise drove them north within two days.

Their needs were simple and baggage was down to backpacks, so they ditched the car and took to the road by Greyhound bus.

With their knees up in the back seat of the second bus they had taken they watched the countryside of South Carolina unfold.

"Would you believe, this is the way I always dreamed of seeing America." Donny said drowsily. "Sounds funny when you think about it. We have been travelling first class for the past weeks right across the country and back, and I feel we have seen more of the country in the past two days than we actually saw during the whole if the earlier trip."

"This is the first time we have not been followed, trailed or otherwise interfered with since we arrived here." Abby wriggled. "That belt holster is digging into my ribs."

Donny moved slightly, and Abby sighed contentedly "That's better," She slipped her hands round his waist and snuggled closer to him.

"Perhaps we could start packing the guns in the bags. After all we only have a few more days to go in America."

"Perhaps you have forgotten that we still do not know what happened to Charles Regret. There are no professional gunmen backing us up now. Karmelian and Karla are in Hawaii now and Jennock? Who knows where Jennock will be now. He is a law unto himself. Anyway we only have ourselves to worry about now, so let's enjoy our final days here before we have to get back to our studies at Uni."

Warm and snug the bus carried them into the evening of the warm Carolina night and their night stop at Charlestown.

They spent three days in the Charlestown area, travelling on foot and by local bus and horse carriage. The charming historic city wove a spell that they found exciting and the combination of the birthplace of modern America, at Fort Sumter where the first shots of the Civil war were fired. The Ante-bellum buildings made a refreshing change to the mainly brash collection of modern buildings that make up the average American town.

Charles Regret limped over to the bar in his New York apartment. He swore as he poured out the tonic water, collected the four pills he had been prescribed by the doctor who had treated him on Santa Catalina, and threw them into his mouth, washing them down with the tonic water. He grimaced at the taste and cursed the injuries that had left him in his present state. Stepping into the freezer cabinet when the explosions started had seemed like a good idea at the time. But the battle to get the door open when he was bobbing about in the sea afterwards had been nearly too much for him.

When the fishing boat had finally picked him up he had been short of oxygen for longer than was good for him and the injuries he had sustained from being thrown about in the cabinet during the explosion had not benefitted from the prolonged oxygen lack.

He turned and looked out of the window at the busy street far below. He was on the twentieth floor of the apartment block and it was one of the many places he had retained when he was at the bank, for just such a use. Here he was unknown and otherwise unremarked. There were all the needed things to keep him in touch with events and, despite the huge personal losses he had sustained, he was still able to access funds for the financing of his search for the people responsible for his current situation.

Though he was well aware of the part played by Karmelian, Jennock and Karla, it was the

British pair that he really blamed for his problems. Without their input the others would all be dead by now and he would not be tottering around on sticks.

His train of thought was interrupted by the beep from his computer. He turned and carefully made his way to the equipment-lined wall and seated himself at the computer terminal.

The Skype message came from one of his team of watchers.

"What?" Regret demanded.

"I found the British pair," The speaker was a small weasel-like man, dressed in the sort of clothing that everyone seemed to wear these days. T-shirt, jeans and trainers.

"Where are they and where are you?" Regret was impatient and almost immediately regretted his impatience. "Sorry, Reilly. I'm not having a good day. What can you tell me?"

Mollified, the little man explained. "I haven't actually seen them but I know where they have been staying. The landlady tells me that they are going up to Jersey, and they are planning to fly out back to Britain in two weeks' time. They want to spend time in New York before they return home."

"Can you find out where they are staying in Jersey?"

"I got that covered, sir, but this has cost me money so far…" His voice trailed off as the signal on his cell was interrupted.

Regret grimaced—money everything was money. "I will have an envelope for you at the drop in Queens by this evening. Good enough?"

"That will be fine, thank you. I am in New York at the moment. I will be in touch when I have news for you."

Regret called out, and a man entered the room, clad in an apron. "Put $500 in an envelope for the Queens dead letter drop, Watson." Regret spoke brusquely, and turned back to the computer.

David Watson looked at the back of his employer. The expression on his face mirrored his thought at the time. He was not a happy man. However, he bit back the comment he would like to have made and settled for, "Yes Sir!" Then he turned and left the room.

In the kitchen of the apartment Watson opened the bread bin and withdrew a handful of twenty and fifty dollar bills. He counted out $500 and placed them in an envelope which he sealed. He picked up the internal phone to the garage below.

"Albert, I'm sending an envelope down the chute. Deliver it to the Queens drop, please."

Albert repeated the instruction back and rang off. Watson then folded the envelope and placed it in a tube-shaped container, which he slotted into the pipe that was mounted against the wall. He shut the cover and with a hiss the container started its journey to the basement.

The cell phone rang and Donny picked up. Abby was in the shower. "Yes?" he said.

"Donny, thank goodness I am in time. Is Abby with you?" Karmelian sounded anxious.

"Abby is here. She is in the shower. What is wrong? Are you and Karla alright?"

"We are alright. But I was worried about you. I've just had a call from Jennock. Regret is alive and he has a call out for Abby and you. Jennock thinks he is in New York, with blood in his eye. We are arriving in Jersey International in three hours. Jennock will be with you shortly. Are you still armed?"

"Yes. We both have our Walther's. But why are you all coming, won't it make it easier for them to find us?"

"We were coming anyway—to make sure you left this country before you got us involved in world war three. Jennock had arranged to join us to see you off. He came across an old friend. The friend mentioned that your names were on someone's shit list. When the story came out, it seems Regret escaped the explosions on the yacht by climbing into a freezer cabinet. It floated apparently and it protected him from the explosions but he got banged about anyway. The door jammed and he suffered from anoxia. His body is still crippled and his brain is impaired from the effects, and it could be years before he gets complete mobility back. That's if he ever does. He blames you two for the whole mess." Karmelian stopped and listened to someone else for a few moments. "Ditch the cell phone now! Smash it. Drown it. Karla reckons they can find you from the GPS signal. Jennock will bring you other phones. Karla is calling him now. Get off the line and don't answer any callers you don't know." Karmelian rang off. Donny tossed the cell phone in the bathroom sink and turned on the taps.

Abby opened the shower screen and poked her head out. "What's happening? I thought I heard the phone."

"You did. It was Karmelian. Regret is still alive and after our blood. Get dressed in a hurry. Jennock is on the way and we need to be pre-pared."

Abby slammed the screen door and stepped out of the shower picking up her towel and rub-bing herself down in front of her appreciative partner. "Stop staring and make sure both guns are in proper shape. Shoo. Out of here."

Reluctantly, Donny left the bathroom, collected the guns and spare ammo and started checking them over.

Jennock arrived shortly after Abby finished her shower. She answered the door at his knock with the towel wrapped round her head, and a gun in her hand. Having let Jennock in, she turned to him and kissed his cheek. "Thanks for coming," she said. "We would have had no idea that Regret survived if you hadn't learned about it and passed it on. Karmelian and Karla are on their way."

"Good. We need back-up if Regret does what he always did, and employs more than one layer of hit men." He grinned, a little shamefaced as the circumstances of their first meeting occurred to him. Shrugging, he said, "Where is Donny?"

Donny answered quietly. "I'm right behind you."

Jennock swung round as Donny thrust his hand out and caught Jennock's instant reaction to hearing the voice behind him.

"Sorry, Jennock. I forgot your hair trigger reactions."

Jennock relaxed. "My fault, living on my own too much, I guess."

The phone rang and all three looked at each other. "It must be Karmelian." Abby said no one else knows where we are."

She lifted the room telephone, "Hello!" For a moment she listened then said, "Hold it. The others should hear this." She pressed the speakerphone button. "OK. Go ahead, Shirley."

The voice of the woman that Donny and Abby knew as Shirley Susskind was clear and a little rushed.

"Look, you two. I know you have no reason to trust me after that little episode earlier on this year. But believe me I was just doing an acting job that I could not afford to turn down. Any way here it is. Some guy has put the word out for information on the location of two British people, man and woman, names Donny Weston and Abby Marshall. Five thousand dollars reward, no questions asked. One of my friends works at your hotel and remembered the names. He rang up to claim the reward before he spoke to me. He mentioned it when he went out to collect. He hasn't come back. Hang on. Someone is breaking in. I am out of here."

Abby called, "Shirley, come here. We'll look after you."

At the other end the phone hit the floor and there were crashing noises. Then nothing!

"Damn, damn, damn. Do you think she heard me?" Abby looked worried. "Those bastards breaking in after her."

Donny said, "We don't know that. Wait and see. We have no idea where she was when she phoned. If she heard then she may well come here. At least she knew where we are."

"Who the hell is she?" Jennock asked.

"Abby, you explain. I'll scout around and see if anything is happening around the hotel."

"Jennock, have you got phones for us?"

"Phones? Yeah, Karmelian said to get two." He rummaged in his jacket pocket and tossed two pay-as-you-go phones onto the bed.

Donny picked one up and passed it to Abby. "Numbers are on the cards." Jennock commented.

Donny took a note of Abby's number, pocketing the cell phone he said, "'I'll be back," trying for the Arnold Schwarzenegger accent and failing miserably. He left to reconnoitre the lobby and the approaches to the hotel.

From the lobby, Donny watched the cab stop and observed the woman he knew as Shirley Susskind arrive. Apart from her purse she was wearing a tank-top and mini skirt, a little under dressed for the current cool weather.

He couldn't help admiring the shapely legs and trim figure as she trotted up the steps to the hotel foyer.

She spotted him standing beside the elevators and came straight over, leaning up to kiss him, almost on the lips. "Wow, you are looking fit," she said breathlessly. "Can we get out of sight? I don't think I was followed, but I cannot be sure."

Donny took her arm and stepped into the elevator. He pressed the button for the top floor and three other floors. When they got out of the elevator on the fourth floor, he checked. There was no one there, so they took the stairs down to the floor below where their room was located.

Abby took charge when they arrived, introducing Jennock. Then turning to Shirley she said "Right. Now, what do we call you?"

Shirley looked a guilty, then shrugged. "My name is Mary-Ann Soutar. I am studying for my degree in acting and stagecraft, at Julliard School, here in New York. I was paid to impersonate Shirley Susskind. It was supposed to be a joke. The kidnap was real. I knew nothing about it. When the guns started going off I nearly flipped. But you seemed to have the whole situation in hand, so I played along."

"What about the call to your supposed father?" Donny put in.

"What was I supposed to do? I was playing the part, so I played it to the full. I should have saved myself the bother. I never did get paid."

Abby said, "Look. The situation here is that there are a bunch of guys out for revenge. Sorry, I'll amend that. There is one guy after revenge. The others are performing for money, but they are just as lethal. What we will do is go after the man Charles Regret. With him out of the way, nobody gets paid. The threat disappears."

"Why is he after you, this guy Regret? What is his angle?" Mary-Ann asked.

"It's a long story, and we are waiting for the rest of the crew so sit down and I'll order up room service while we wait.

Mary-Ann used the bathroom to tidy herself up, and dress a little more comfortably with the help of Abby's wardrobe.

Now, wearing a slightly longer skirt and blouse she sat next to Jennock, ate sandwiches and listened, while Abby brought her up to date.

At the end of the story Abby said, "So you see, you would probably be better off going to stay with your mother for a week or so, and leaving the rest to us. The option is that you may get hurt, and, if we don't win, possibly killed."

"I like your style. You got pushed around for no reason. So you pushed back. On my own I could bring the roof down on my folks. With you guys I feel not quite so helpless. So if it is all right with you, I'll stick around."

Jennock relaxed. He had been a little tense when Mary-Ann started speaking. Now she had made her feelings known he felt happier, and he was unsure why. He was not accustomed to being close to women. The association with Abby and Karla had unsettled a lot of his preconceived notions on the subject. The arrival of Mary-Ann had really been a curve ball as far as he was concerned. He had been with women. Used, might be a better description, always on a temporary basis.

Since the association with Abby, Donny, Karla and Karmelian, his awareness of the opposite sex had undergone a change. His uncertainties were disturbing and they seemed to be centred on Mary-Ann whom he was seriously looking at with unaccustomed feelings.

Abby noticed. Looking at Mary-Ann she realized that Mary-Ann had noticed too. What is more, Mary-Ann did not seem too put off by the interest. She chatted quietly to him, learning that Jennock disliked New York, though he had on occasion worked there. She told him that she loved the place and was due to spend at least one more year there at school. Jennock said nothing to this, but he looked thoughtful.

Well, well! Abby thought. *Could it be that the impassive shell that Jennock presented to the world had been breached?*

The arrival of Karmelian and Karla stirred everyone into activity and after the introductions had been made, they got down to the planning of the campaign to get Regret off their case.

There was a limit to the number of things they could come up with when they did not have a clue where Regret lived. Mary-Ann came up with the solution. "Someone has a contact number otherwise they will not be able to claim the reward. It should not be too difficult to locate the address once we have the telephone number. Should it?"

It took a moment for the idea to sink in. Then Jennock said "I have a contact that has the number." He took out his cell phone and punched in a number. It was answered immediately. The voice said "Where do I collect then."

Jennock spoke quietly, his voice full of menace. "Elroy, my friend, if you wish to survive today, you need to tell me two things, now. First thing- the telephone number for Mr Regret, second- his current address. I'll accept the answers in any order."

The voice of Elroy spluttered on the other end of the phone. "But, Jennock, I don't know where he lives. His telephone number is…" He reeled off a list of numbers that Jennock carefully noted.

"Very good. I will give you until 1500 hours today to come back to me with the address. I'll speak to you later. Bye."

At the other end Elroy looked wasted. He knew where Mr Regret stayed. He made it his business to know. But he was sworn to secrecy by his own self-preservation instincts. If Charles Regret ever got to know that he had passed on his address to an enemy, he would skin him alive. Only if Jennock got to Mr Regret first, would there be no problem. Jennock had not been kidding when he said deliver or else. So Elroy realized that Jennock must get there first.

Having made his mind up Elroy called Jennock. "It's that secure apartment block on 5th Avenue, overlooking the park, the tall white one. The doorkeeper wears the midnight blue uniform and won't let you in without a pass or permission."

Chapter thirteen

The group digested the information Jennock supplied, each in their own way working on the problem of how to stop Regret.

Mary-Ann said, "How about I deliver a message?"

All eyes turned to her. She blushed. "If I dress as a singing telegram and arrive on the doorstep with a message from his old friend, Joe Pastrami, or whoever. I could leave a parcel with something nasty."

She looked around the group. All were shaking their heads. She shrugged.

Jennock said, "I can get in there and from inside I can let others in. The only problem is that we do not know how many men Regret has on duty at any one time."

Donny turned to Jennock. "How do you get inside?"

"The next door block has a common roof with a helipad. They are linked with a bridge for easy access."

"But it will be well guarded. You can count on it," Abby said.

Jennock leaned forward. "I have used the helipad What most people do not realize is that the bridge is built with solid sides and a cable tunnel underneath. It's not big enough to crawl through, but the attaching clamps have room to put a karabiner on each. If I run a rope through from one side to the other, I can get across under the bridge from the floor below the roof. If I do it at night, the corridor window should be clear. If there is a guard at the window, I can neutralise him with a quiet shot. The gap is only twenty-five. Once the rope is in place others can join me in Regret's building."

"But the window, they don't make them easy to open in skyscrapers," Karmelian said. "And if you are hanging about outside trying to use a glass cutter in armored glass, you could still be there the following day."

"One: the glass in those windows will not be armor. It will be standard double-glazing. Two: Because of access to the cable tunnel the window actually has the ability to open so that engineers can gain access to that end of the tunnel. The same applies to the window on the other side. The line of windows for the emergency stairs runs vertically downward below the bridge on each building. The two buildings are actually joined up to the fifteenth floor. The roof of the joined section is ten floors below the bridge. I intend to have sufficient rope to use to abseil down to the roof if necessary. The main fact is that there are no apartment windows on the facing walls of the buildings. All the windows are on stairwells. The only risk is that there will be watchers on the stairwells. I do have an idea to deal with that factor if it arises."

"Who are thinking of using for this little exercise?" Abby wanted to know.

Jennock hesitated, then, "I thought myself, Karmelian and Donny."

"Karla, Mary-Ann and I are expected to sit and wait until our men folk get back. Is that what you had in mind?" There was a dangerous edge to her voice that warned Jennock that the matter would not end here.

He looked at the other two. He got no help there. "I thought that the climb might be difficult for you."

Abby turned her back on the men and looked at Karla, shaking her head slightly but enough to warn Karla.

Karla took the hint and said nothing. Shortly afterwards the three women went to get their hair done, or so they said.

Donny had other ideas but kept them to himself.

The refined plan Jennock had suggested went ahead. All three kitted out with climbing gear navigated the underside of the bridge, while the watchers, unknowing, kept an eye on the bridge itself and the landing pad area which was floodlit. Jennock mounted the stairs to the bridge level and confirmed that there were two men there. He took no chances. His silenced pistol coughed twice. Both men gasped and fell. Karmelian followed and injected both unconscious men.

"They will wake with a hangover and a sore chest." He observed. "That was close range for the vests they were wearing."

Donny had explored downstairs, locating the apartment on the twentieth floor by the two hoods standing guard. When the three men appeared in front of them guns levelled, both shrugged, handed over the weapons and submitted to the plastic handcuffs without a murmur.

Donny started to worry at this point. It all seemed too easy. They tied and gagged the men on the next landing and, using a key found on one of the men, opened the apartment door.

Their silent entrance went undiscovered. The problem was there was no one in there. The apartment was empty. The three intruders were still taking this factor in, when suddenly there were men with guns all around them. The next door apartment had been linked with this one. What appeared to be closet doors actually allowed access to the other apartment. Both doors were now open, and they were all three captured.

Jennock was furious with himself. It had never occurred to him that both apartments were actually being used as one.

Their six captors disarmed them and made them all sit down on the floor. Two of the men went to the apartment door and took the place of the two missing men.

Using his sticks Charles Regret hobbled in. He looked to Donny like a caricature of the urbane banker that he had seen in operation and on board the *Risk.*

The voice was familiar. "Well, gentlemen, where are the ladies? No matter. I will find them and ensure they have a memorable demise. You will already be gone by then, of course. I decided not to shoot you. It occurred to me that having time to contemplate your end was more satisfactory."

Karmelian spoke in a normal voice, calmly and clearly. "You men do realize that this man never pays his debts. He currently owes my colleague here." He indicated Jennock. "And me, two and a half million for services that included killing my other friend here."

Jennock and Donny both nodded.

"If he has not already paid you, I suggest you get payment now. Otherwise the other team outside at present will, as the saying goes, terminate all of you with extreme prejudice."

The leader of the men watching over the prisoners looked at the front door.

Regret clapped his hands slowly. "Well done! Karmelian, is it not?"

All seemed to cool down at this. Only at the door, there was a burst of conversation and then the door opened with a bang and three miniskirted girls in heavy make-up and high heels tottered in waving bottles. The two guards, who had meanwhile rearmed themselves with Ingram SMG's with long magazines rushed in after them. The four gunmen saw the Ingram's and without hesitation shot them both. The bottles carried by the girls suddenly became clubs. The four gunmen watching the prisoners were reduced to two within seconds. A third found a knife at his throat and lost interest in his scheduled task. Their leader was down, choking under the right leg of Jennock. Regret was on his feet tottering backward seemingly unaware how close he was to the open window. Abby threw her bottle at Regret with all her force. She missed. Regret stepped to one side with a sneer on his face. He had dropped one of his sticks and produced a

Glock automatic. He lifted it to shoot at Abby but was off balance. The bullet hit the ceiling as he hit the window-sill behind him. The gun fell as he grabbed for the frame of the window, and missed. He screamed for the entire journey to the sidewalk, when he stopped.

In the room the fight was over. Karla freed the three captives who collected their weapons. Leaving the various bodies where they lay, they left the apartment, and made it to the roof, all six crossing the bridge to the next door building.

In the hotel room once more, the girls, having lost the make-up and dressed once more in their normal clothes, explained how they got past the doorman by appearing in a limo and producing a letter from Charles Regret requesting entertainers for the extra staff he had hired.

It was obviously not the first time it had happened. Karla had been there before and seen it happen.

Jennock offered to make sure that Mary-Ann was able to reoccupy her apartment safely. Karmelian looked at him in astonishment, but kept his mouth shut when he noticed Karla shaking her head at him.

Mary-Ann looked at Jennock seriously. "I thought you did not like New York. You couldn't wait to get back to the West Coast."

He hesitated. "I think maybe I misjudged the place somewhat, possibly because I didn't know anyone here. I am willing to give it a few days and see if I was wrong. That is if I can find someone to show me around."

"I can arrange that. But first let's see if I can get my apartment sorted out. You can shake down on the couch tonight if you like. We'll sort something out tomorrow."

Mary-Ann turned to the others who were standing stunned at the performance happening in front of them. "I'll take Jennock off your hands, and we'll see how things go. Thank you for allowing me to help. I enjoyed it." She kissed both Donny and Karmelian.

Both of the girls kissed her goodbye and promised to be in touch if, and when, they ever came to New York. A red-faced Jennock under-went similar treatment from Abby and Karla, and shook hands with the other men.

As they left the room, Abby heard Mary-Ann say, "What is your first name. I cannot keep calling you Jennock?"

She did not hear his reply.

Epilogue....

The Virgin Atlantic Jumbo landed on time at London Heathrow, and both of them were tired and ready to crash out for a few days.

"Why is it, when we return from holiday, we need to take a rest to get over it?" Donny said with a sigh.

"Probably has something to do with him," Abby said, as she pointed out the smiling face of Jonathon Glynn, waiting at the exit beyond the baggage claim.

~*~*~

David O'Neil

~*~*~

Other titles in O'Neil's Abby Marshall and Donny Weston thriller series:

*****A Thrill a Minute*****
*****Fatal Meeting*****
*****Just One Thing After Another*****
*****Lethal Complications*****

~*~*~

Titles in O'Neil's Counterstroke series
*****Exciting, Isn't It?*****
*****Market Forces*****

Other adventure books by David O'Neil
*****The Mercy Run*****

All titles available on line, at better book stores or at A-Argus Better Book Publishers. Also available in ebook form.
www.a-argusbooks.com

www.ingramcontent.com/pod-product-compliance
Lightning Source LLC
Chambersburg PA
CBHW051653260626
47170CB00004B/1489